HOLLOW
BOOK ONE OF THE SCORPION CHRONICLES

RUSSELL TURNBULL

RUSSELL TURNBULL STUDIOS

Russell Turnbull Studios
Carlisle, Pennsylvania

Second Edition
Trade Paperback ISBN: 979-8989088508

Cover designed by Miblart.

THE SCORPION CHRONICLES

Hollow: Book One

Dark: Book Two

Vast: Book Three

This book is for Alysen Kathleen Turnbull.
I love you, Aly Kat!

CONTENTS

AUTHOR'S NOTES

You will undoubtedly find some strange words within the pages of this book.

Most–if not all–of these strange words are derived from a dialect of a much older form of the English language that has been all but forgotten by modern man. Some, however, have come from an even older dialect of French, Norse, Classic Greek and Latin, among others.

For example: Our hero's name, "Thunor" is actually the Old English word for Thunder, while the King's name, "Lagu Ofer'Eal" is Old English as well and means: (Lagu) Law, (Ofer) Over, (Eal) All.

As I stated before, each strange word has an actual meaning, as do all of the names of the locations and creatures. The names of each describe what the owner of the name is about.

The dream sequence in Chapter Four: Hydan Seir (Hidden Shire) is an actual dream I had the night before I wrote that part of the story. I was compelled to add it into the book (I hope it works!)

The lyrics to the song: "Xobish" also within Hydan Seir, vaguely go to the tune found in Monty Python & the Holy Grail – "Sir Robin." I enjoyed this film immensely.

Thanks Eric, John, Terry, Terry and the late, great Graham (& Neil.) Apologies to those whom I missed.

Special thanks go out to Mr. Stephen King* and Mr. R. A. Salvatore...

... Thank you both for your inspiration and company. You were always there (in book form) for me when I needed you the most on all of those lonely nights.

Thanks Michele, your edits are "Golden."

A very special thanks goes out to my (new) wife, Tania: I love you Baby. Thank you OH so much for being my muse and never giving up on me and for giving me all of those pushes to keep going whenever I started to give up on myself.

Ultimately, without you, this book or any that follow, (and there will be more) would never have come to be.

Thank YOU... Yeah, YOU.

You're reading this, so that means that you're interested in it enough to read this part of the book.

Without YOU, future books would not be possible, so keep reading and...

ENJOY!!

Russell Turnbull

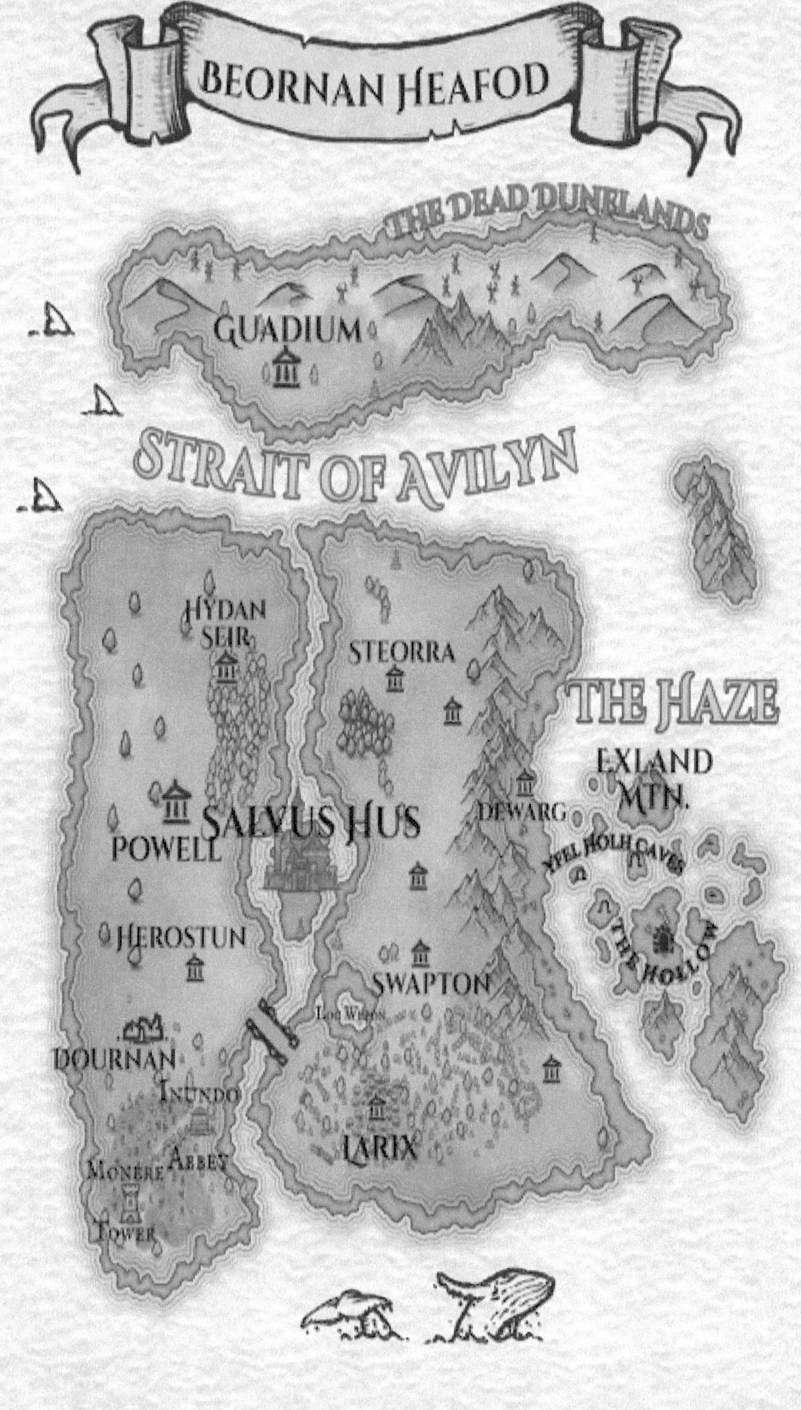

BEORNAN HEAFOD
THE DEAD DUNELANDS
GUADIUM
STRAIT OF AVILYN
HYDAN SEIR
STEORRA
THE HAZE
EXLAND MTN.
POWELL
SALVUS HUS
DEWARG
NYEL HOLH CAVES
THE HOLLOW
HEROSTUN
SWAPTON
Low Woods
DOURNAN
INUNDO
LARIX
MONERE ABBEY
TOWER

PROLOGUE

'What's *that?*' I asked myself as I crouched down and held my position behind a large oak tree. 'Humans are not supposed to be in the enchanted Seolfer Wudu, homeland of the elven race, especially human *children!*' My thoughts continued as I peered at a young human boy that looked lost and alone.

The boy was crying and walking around aimlessly.

He must have wandered away from the small party of humans I had seen a few days ago near Loch Wepan.

The boy looked scared as he walked slowly through the trees, calling something out in his own language over and over again.

I could not speak the common tongue of humans yet and I was unsure of how I should handle this situation.

My father was human and I was wishing I had learned his language when I had the chance, but he was gone now.

My father had died in a small skirmish between the elves and the orcs less than a year ago.

I decided that I had to take action, lest the child wanders off and discovers our village of Larix.

I hid my longbow and held my hands out so the child could see that they were empty.

I then took the first of many steps of faith toward the scared human child, trying to get his attention without frightening the poor creature any more than he already was.

He saw me and instantly ran for me with his arms wide open.

If elves and humans had been at war, this child would not have survived.

CHAPTER ONE

THE GATHERING

I was woken up by the sound of a sharp knocking on my front door.

The sun was just barely beginning to crest the mountains in the far northeast.

Less than a minute later, the knocking resumed and made my eyes spring open again.

There was more relentless knocking. *'This had better be important,'* I thought as I slowly raised my head from the pillow.

"Take ease!" I called sharply to the closed door, and then there was the sound of shuffling feet from behind the door.

There was more knocking, progressively louder and harder.

I was beginning to suspect that whoever it was would break my door down.

Even more knocking, "Mr. McLaaud..." A voice called, impatiently.

Reluctantly, I rose from my bed and stumbled to the door.

The floor was cold, hard and dusty.

There was still more knocking, "*Mr. McLaaud!*"

The voice was agitated.

(So was I.)

I grabbed the crystal dagger from the shelf beside the door, cracked the door ajar and saw a royal messenger from Salvus Hus, the royal city on the island of Cynings.

The messenger was peering in at me with an impatient and annoyed look on his face.

I rolled my eyes and tossed the crystal dagger back onto its shelf, sighed and opened the door wide enough for the messenger to enter.

"I was under the impression that elves never slept," the messenger stated as he observed me yawning and stretching.

He rudely pushed his way into my home and looked around as if he was some sort of inspector.

He looked as if he was disgusted with what he saw.

"I'm half human, mister..." I prodded, yawning again.

"Mitterer," he answered, "Royal messenger to his majesty, Lagu Ofer'Eal, ruler of all Beornan Heafod," he announced quite arrogant-ly.

"Aren't you proud?" I muttered sarcastically under my breath, and then said audibly, "So, to what do I owe this (cough) honor?"

"You have been summoned by His Majesty to embark on an important mission." He stopped.

I just stood there blinking, looking at him and waiting for more until a minute or two passed, and then I asked, "A mission?"

"The details will be revealed to you by His Majesty once you arrive on the island. That is all I can tell you," Mitterer said as he handed me a written fiat from the King.

"Inform the King that I accept and that I shall arrive by nightfall tomorrow, or sooner," I said.

Mitterer nodded, bowed low and then left.

I closed the door, leaned my back against it, listened for the sound of his horse's hooves to fade away and then sighed. *'What did I just get myself into?'* I asked myself in a thought.

I also had the thought to go back to sleep, but then decided against it and started to gather up my weapons, armor and whatever else I needed for this mysterious mission the young King wanted me to go on.

After a quick meal, I journeyed outside to prepare my prized horse, a black roan stallion named Stahvee, for the upcoming adventure.

It occurred to me at that very moment that I had neglected to inquire as to how and why I, of all people, had been chosen to embark on a mission for the young King.

I *did* have many years of prior training as a ranger, but so did many other people in this area of the realm.

Perhaps my name had been drawn from some sort of a lottery?

Stahvee was patiently waiting, as always, in his corral slowly trotting around his fenced in area.

His pace quickened as he saw my approach.

The roan raised his head and raised his legs higher into a proud prance.

I could almost see a smile on his face.

I reached the gate, opened it and then entered the corral.

Stahvee circled me as if to say *'Hello!'*

I reached out to caress his snout and he slowed to a stop eagerly allowing my hand to touch his soft face.

An hour later, Stahvee and I were on our way to the nearest ferry dock, South Ferian Harbor, then to South Port Royale, the Port on the southern edge of Cynings Island.

Salvus Hus, the castle, stood in the center of the island.

As we rode along the trail, the sun was rising higher in the sky, spreading its warming glow across the newly thawed land.

The last traces of frost had been expelled days before.

The hibernating animals would soon be poking their heads sleepily from their dens.

Nature's colorful spectrum would soon follow in full glorious grandeur.

The chill air was progressively warming as the hours passed by and songbirds sang glorious tunes that only they (and the druids) could understand, in the surrounding, still bare trees.

Just ahead, I could barely make out some movement on the trail, the open plains before me stretched on as far as the eye could see.

We slowly, cautiously continued forward to observe a large group of fairies and a sprite, gathered by a dirt track of sorts.

Some of the fairies were mounted upon the backs of rabbits as if the rabbits were horses, and were waiting in a row, side by side in a line.

As I approached, the row of mounted rabbits quickly sprinted away from the line that was drawn in the dirt and raced around on a circular track, while the rest of the fairies cheered on and made bets.

The cheering continued as I slowed to a stop to observe the odd little race.

The mounted rabbits raced on faster as they rounded the dirt track a number of times.

The cheering grew louder as the race continued.

The mounted rabbits raced faster and faster until the final lap had ended.

A brown and white speckled bunny claimed victory and gold was exchanged to the winner.

I continued on my way with a smile on my face as the sounds of a new race trailed off behind me.

After a few more miles, we entered an area dotted by small houses and huts.

Busy human people, dressed in common tunics and work worn rags, went on about their own business performing daily chores of tending to chickens, pigs, goats, sheep and cows.

A few others were busy mending a broken fence that looked as if it had been damaged in a recent scuffle with perhaps an orc raiding party the night before.

Off in the near distance laid the trading town of Swapton.

The sounds of blacksmiths and the faint smells of food wafted around carried on the slight mid-morning breeze.

The trail forked off to the left quite a few yards before the gates of Swapton, so I veered off to the left and continued to take the path to the harbor.

The sun had passed overhead and began to lean toward the west; South Ferian Harbor was then visible to the north.

After a few moments of a hard northbound gallop, I could see that the waters of Loch Regalis were icy blue and the closer Stahvee and I got to it, the cooler and cooler the breeze became as it traveled over the waves.

The sunlight had begun to dim the further and longer we rode and it was twilight by the time I arrived on the docks of South Ferian Harbor.

The day's last ferry to South Port Royale was almost finished loading up its final passengers; I had made it just in time.

I paid the ferryman and boarded the boat.

I purchased a feedbag of oats and grain for Stahvee and strapped it to his snout; the boat shoved off and we were on our way.

The breeze calmed down, the torches flickered less and the waves smoothed out making for a calm, enjoyable ride to the island.

Across the reach, I could barely make out the shape of Salvus Hus Castle looming in the fading light.

It grew larger and larger the closer we got to it, anxiety gripped at me as thoughts of wonder filled my head; we drifted on.

The decks were lit by flickering torches and groups of passengers cast long shadows as they mingled amongst themselves.

"E's got te be a fast one, 'e does!" A dwarf remarked as he strolled out of the shadows and pointed at Stahvee.

Two more dwarves stepped out of those same shadows and joined him.

The small group of dwarves took a few steps closer to admire my horse in some better light and my hand automatically touched the hasp of my trusty sword.

"What makes you say that?" I inquired politely.

"Ye kin tell by th' beastie's muscular flanks, Elf," the dwarf answered, smiling.

He was the average in dwarven height of four and a half foot tall with graying red hair on both his head and his face.

He was wearing light plate mail armor over a suit of thick leather and his weapon of choice was a Great Axe that looked as if it had seen and survived a great many battles.

I noticed that Stahvee had finished his feed, so I removed the bag and dusted off his snout.

"He can hold his own," I conceded and ran my fingers through his thick, long mane.

"Me thinks more than that!" The dwarf countered with a smile as the three looked in admiration for a moment longer, and then ambled away with departing nods.

I watched them go, and then turned to the front of the boat to gauge our progress; Salvus Hus was only a short way away by then, so I mounted my horse and slowly moved toward the exit.

A moment later, I was on the dirt trail that led to the gates of Salvus Hus.

The dirt path was smooth and not as deeply worn as the paths and trails on the mainland.

The grounds around the path were beautifully landscaped, from what I could see in the dark, as my infrared elven sight was not as good as that of my full blooded cousins, yet even in the dark I could tell that there were flowers everywhere just from the fragrance in the air.

Somewhere off to my right, I could hear the steady trickle from a small waterfall pouring over smooth rocks into a small pond, while the constant call of a very close whippoorwill echoed through my head.

A few yards ahead, torchlight illuminated the gates that guarded the entrance to the walled town and courtyard.

I dismounted and led my horse to the gates, then stopped as a large guard wearing shining royal blue and silver plate mail armor, wielding a halberd, stepped forward and raised his hand high in the air, "Please state your name and business," he politely droned.

"I am Thunor McLaaud of Larix, here with an official fiat from His majesty, Lord Lagu Ofer'Eal," I announced and held out the document that the royal messenger had given me.

The guard scanned down a list he had, looked up at me and then said, "Welcome to Salvus Hus," he bowed low, "We are honored."

I bowed in return and Stahvee followed suit as I had trained him, we then passed through the gates and entered the town.

I overheard the guard comment in awe to his partner about Stahvee's talent.

Beyond the gates, the courtyard opened into a well torch lit area with flowers and bright shrubberies that donned the landscape along with fruit trees, oddly, already in bloom so early in the season.

The grand castle loomed straight ahead at the end of the long cobblestone walkway.

"Greetings, late traveler," a voice to my right grabbed my attention.

An older gentleman wearing work clothes and high boots, a leather apron and a straw hat, quickly strode up to my side and continued talking, "I am Festus, the stableman, may I take care of your horse?"

"He just ate on the ferry," I said as I handed him Stahvee's reins.

"I'll see that he gets a good rub down and brushing," he said. "May I interest you in a room at the inn?" He asked. "I'm assuming you'll need your rest if you're going to see the King tomorrow."

I agreed and followed him into the stable.

From a small desk, he produced a key and handed it to me.

I offered him some money but he refused, telling me that any guest of the King's is honored and shall not pay.

I left some gold on the desk before I began to walk to the door.

"Now you'll be wanting a meal and perhaps a drink or two," he called to me as I reached the door; I stopped and turned to face him, then nodded.

He pointed to the tavern across the street, 'The Broken Blade.' I thanked him and I was on my way.

<hr>

As soon as I entered the dimly lit tavern, the smell of roasted beef hit me in the stomach like a giant balled-up fist.

I took a quick, thorough look around as I walked up to the bar and noticed six large, circular tables with six chairs ringing them.

There was a table in each corner and two in the center of the room.

Upon entering, the service bar was over on the right side of the room and lined the entire wall.

Directly across from the bar was a huge natural fieldstone fireplace.

The room looked unoccupied except for four human men, three wearing common tunics, the fourth wearing a suit of light plate mail armor, each enjoying a meal and drinks.

They were seated at the center table closest to the fire.

I got the barmaid's attention, and then walked past the men to sit at the corner table furthest away from the door.

As I passed the men, the one in the armor, a knight, looked up at me, did a double take, and then continued eating his meal with a thoughtful look on his face.

My table was the closest table to the nice, warm, crackling fire.

As I sat waiting, I overheard bits and pieces of their conversation about an upcoming hunt for orc raiders near a town called Dournan; it held no real interest for me.

Finally, at my table, the barmaid took my order of a meal of roast beef and ale, and then disappeared into the kitchen.

The men continued with their adventurous tales, and quite quickly the barmaid returned with my drink.

The fire crackled in the fireplace and sent a warm glow around the room, casting long, dancing shadows everywhere.

I took a long pull from my pint of ale and relaxed in my chair.

The knight from the other table got up from his chair, bid his companions a good night, saying that he had a very busy day ahead of him tomorrow, took a long look at me and then casually strode out the door.

A pine knot popped in the fire and the logs slightly shifted, sending orange floating embers up the chimney, and sap from deep within the wood hissed as it cooked.

As I sat and nursed my ale, the door abruptly opened and the three dwarves from the ferry entered and bellied up to the bar.

I began to wonder what they were doing there, but quickly decided that it was none of my business and dismissed my thoughts as trivial.

I turned to stare at the glowing fire for a short time and in what seemed to me to be a very short while, the barmaid returned with my meal and fresh ale.

I ate in silence, watching the flames seductively dance, hypnotizing me.

At the bar, the dwarves sat and drank, conversing amongst one another while the men bid a familiar goodnight to the barmaid and barkeep and slowly departed.

I finished my meal and lazily observed the fire while I slowly sipped my ale.

I then got up, tossed a few coins to the barmaid and turned toward the door to leave.

"We serve a very filling breakfast at sun-up," the barmaid called to me as I reached the exit.

I turned to the barmaid, smiled, and then noticed the horse- admiring dwarf give me a nod.

I narrowed my eyes, nodded back and then exited the tavern out into the night.

Outside, as I walked from 'The Broken Blade' to the inn, I concentrated my gaze toward the castle that loomed before me in the dark.

A light in the window at the top of the tall minaret caught my eye as I thought I saw the silhouette of a young woman, but my quick double-take suggested a visual error.

I arrived at the inn, climbed the stairs to my room and quietly approached my door; I carefully listened, my hand rested on the hasp of my sword.

Satisfied that the coast was clear, I slipped the key into the lock, slowly turned it and then eased the door open.

A low flame danced within the glass of a lantern on the bedside table giving off just enough light to assure me that the room was safe, secure and empty.

I entered the room and closed and locked the door.

I set aside my gear, climbed upon the bed and settled in for a much needed rest.

My mind floated free; it wandered around and I slowly drifted off to sleep, while vivid dreams switched from the short journey to the castle, to dreams of the odd rabbit race, to visions of that spectral silhouette and then to memories of the three dwarves that I had met on the ferry, and then again at the tavern.

Behind the pictures that were flashing through my mind, I could see orange embers floating up into a vast nothingness.

The phantasmagoria continued into the early morning hours and I was left in a slight state of unrest as the sun came up.

A rooster crowed.

Reluctantly, I chose to stay awake, so I rose from my bed, strapped my gear back on and headed back to 'The Broken Blade' for some breakfast.

On the way, I was intercepted by Festus, the stableman.

I smiled as he stopped me and I shook his hand. "How's my horse?" I asked.

"He is certainly enjoying his stay," he answered. "He has taken a grand liking to one of the mares I have boarded as well."

I handed him a few more coins and thanked him again.

He smiled and went into the cabin adjoining the stables, perhaps to have his own breakfast, and I continued on to 'The Broken Blade.'

The tavern was reasonably empty at such an early hour of the morning and both the barkeep and the barmaid were busy cooking and cleaning.

The barkeep himself greeted me with a smile as I sat where I was the night before.

"Welcome, honored guest," the barkeep called, "what can I get for you?"

"Whatever you've got cooking," I yawned.

"Would you like light honey mead with that?" He suggested.

I nodded and sank into my chair as he retreated back into the kitchen to fix my order.

I sat, swimming within my own mind, reflecting on the strange dreams from the night before.

Fairie mounted rabbits cavorted through my visions, what a strange event to just *happen* upon—

"Ye look like ye've na' rested in *ages,*" a voice said, shattering my thoughts, "if I'd na' seen ye' leave wi' me own two eyeballs last night, me self would be thinkin' ye'd na' left that chair atoll!"

I looked up to see the slightly recognizable dwarf from the ferry, standing before me. "Might me self join ye?"

"Be my guest," I said and motioned for him to take a seat.

"I be Balt Copperbottom of Dewarg," The dwarf announced with a low bow.

He leaned his Great Axe against the neighboring chair and took his seat.

"Well met," I said as I nodded low, "I'm called Thunor McLaaud of Larix in Seolfer Wudu; half-elf."

"Aye," the dwarf laughed, "ye looked a wee bit *mixed* in me own eyeballs."

The barmaid arrived with my meal and drink and Balt ordered the same thing.

The dwarf put enough gold on the table to pay for both of our meals twice over.

The barmaid scooped up the coins with a big smile and thanked him.

I offered to pay him back, but he waved it off with his hand.

The barmaid immediately returned with the dwarf's order.

"Are you here to see the King?" I asked, breaking the ice.

"I be here with a fiat, yet I've no idea why," he admitted.

"As with I," I said.

⚬

"That makes three of us," a new voice announced, "may I join you as well?" Sitting in the far corner, hidden within the shadows appeared a female elf that was wearing an earth tone blended cloak over padded leather armor; the rest of her gear besides a longbow was hidden under her cloak.

She stood up and approached our table.

I stretched out my open hand and waved it in an arc over an open chair as if to say, '*sit.*'

"Th' more th' merrier," Balt quipped.

She sat down and announced, "I am Loher D'Rolwynn, also of Seolfer Wudu," then she looked directly at me, winked and then said, "full elf." A beautiful smile appeared upon her lips.

Balt drained his mug, and then said, "We all be here on behest of th' King, yet we know na' why."

"I'm quite convinced we shall find out the reason shortly," Loher offered.

"We should all go to see the King together," I suggested.

The others agreed and Balt ordered a round of drinks to celebrate our new fellowship.

We sat and got to know each other over a round or two of drinks, but oddly enough, no one became intoxicated in the slightest.

Loher began one conversation by asking, "What skills do we each possess that differs from those of each other's skills?"

"Well," I began, "I have trained to be a ranger for well over half of my life."

"At th' risk o' soundin' conceded, I, meself, 'ave na' been bested in a fight in a good three hunnerd year'er more," the dwarf admitted with a belch.

"Well apparently," Loher began, "we have been called here to be together for a reason, so I may as well tell you that there has been no lock so far that I have not been able to pick and no trap set so far that I have not been able to disarm or get around. There is also nothing that is not affixed to a stable surface that I cannot steal, yes, I *am* a thief."

Loher then knocked her knuckles on the wooden tabletop and spit over her right shoulder to ward off any jinxes.

"Ye be none too shabby at hidin' yerself either," Balt added with an accepting grin.

The she-elf blushed.

"So, we are a group of... a ranger, a fighter and a thief." I observed.

"I prefer the term 'rogue'," Loher laughed.

"It seems to me that the King might be forming some sort of faction or militia," I guessed.

"Aye, but te what end?" Balt wondered out loud.

As the morning stretched on and turned into midday, we sat and pondered our questions, slowly turning our discussion into vague self histories.

We shared a midday meal and enjoyed jovial laughter; those who were once complete strangers that morning had become closer friends by that afternoon.

A Royal Guard dressed in bluish tinted armor suddenly entered the tavern, looked around the tavern and then approached our table, "His Royal Majesty, King Lagu Ofer'Eal summons you to join him in the castle at once," the Royal Guard boldly announced, handed the barkeep a large purse of coins and then motioned for us to follow him out through the courtyard and up to the castle.

The courtyard was alive with townsfolk.

A bazaar was set up and a small group of minstrels was playing a jaunty tune about some sort of large beelike creature.

Children danced and played around a jester that was walking on his hands in a wide circle.

As we were led through the open castle doors, the music and merriment swiftly faded and the air took on a more regal ambiance.

The chamber beyond the doors widened to a gaping passage that led up a dozen stairs to a large, ornately carved wooden door.

The arabesque took up the entire center of the door.

The walls, floor and ceiling of the chamber were a shimmering, pristine white and gold colored marble.

As we reached the top step, another guard pulled open the large ornate door to expose the grand throne room.

This room was also the same white and gold marble, and the throne was made of a rich jade that almost looked out of place.

A long red runner ran from the door where we stood, up to the foot of the throne, upon which the King himself sat; he was a young human boy no older than the age of twelve, frail and skinny.

Long, flowing blond hair hung from his head and hung loosely over his shoulders and his eyes were of the deepest blue, like that of the summer sky on a hot humid day.

At the risk of being disrespectful and to be completely honest, it was quite difficult to determine whether I was looking at a boy or a girl; I found myself in extreme unease with this unwanted discovery.

The guard led us before the young ruler and we all bowed low as the King slowly rose to his feet.

"Please rise," the King said quickly before we even got half way down through our bow; he was making a rapid upward motion with his hands, an embarrassed look upon his face, "Get up, get up, get up," he half chuckled, half groaned. "Send in the others," he said to the guard.

"As you wish, my Liege," the guard said as he bowed, and then he clicked his heels, spun around sharply, and exited the room.

The young King shuddered with a deep frown on his face as the guard disappeared through the doorway, "I detest such useless and ancient formalities," he groaned.

Stunned, we all looked around at each other in confusion.

"T'is a difficult habit for your loyal subjects to break, Your Majesty," a human knight called, as he and a plump little halfling entered the room.

The young ruler's face lit up with a grand smile, "Welcome back, Sir Quinn and Brother Atlberry," the King greeted with open arms, "I trust you had a safe journey."

"Indeed, we did, Your Highness," the halfling priest affirmed and obviously oppressed a habitual bow.

The knight, whom I had recognized from the tavern the night before, took a quick study of the three of us newcomers, "We seem to be missing the wi—", he began, but was cut off.

As if on cue, there was a loud *pop* and a large puff of pinkish smoke appeared just in front of the throne.

I quickly drew my sword, not knowing at the time what was happening, but as the smoke cleared, we all observed an extremely attractive human female wearing grey robes, with long flowing fiery red hair that surrounded her neck and shoulders.

The young King laughed and gave her a warm hug, "Meeka always *loves* to make a dramatic entrance, don't you, Meeka?"

Meeka just smiled a big toothy grin, batted her eyelashes and nodded her head.

———◆———

"Now that we are all here," the King began, "Let us adjourn to the sitting room."

"Please," Meeka offered, "allow me."

More pinkish smoke surrounded us, along with another loud *pop!*

As the smoke cleared, we each found ourselves standing next to a chair around a long table that was headed by the young King, who seemed utterly amused by the mystic magical display.

The King began as we all took our seats, "As you all know, but I shall state again, I am Lagu Ofer'Eal, reigning ruler of all Beornan Heafod." He looked to his right at Sir Quinn, "Good Sir Knight—"

The knight stood up from his chair and swept his gaze over his audience, "I am Sir Seth Quinn, Royal Knight of Salvus Hus." He then looked to *his* right at the halfling, and then took his seat again.

The halfling stood on the chair so he could see over the table, "My name is Brother Fost Atlberry, a cleric from the temple of Onh. I hail from the hidden Hydan Seir, in the meadows of Leah." The halfling then bowed low and plopped down on his butt in his chair.

The mysterious red-haired woman stood and continued, "Meeka Ashpin of Guadium, at your service," she said as she slyly looked around, produced a large white mouse from the folds of her robes, and then let the creature loose upon the table.

The wizard, Meeka's voice continued from the mouth of the rodent that now stood in the center of the table, "I studied the magic arts from none other than the great Wizard Ficolus, atop the Exland Mountain in Haze Cove!" The mouse stopped, stood on its hind feet, and was rapidly enveloped in a bright concentrated flash of light and vanished.

(Poof! - Applause.)

The introductions continued.

Balt, the dwarven fighter went next, and Loher the elven rogue followed.

Finally, it was my turn and I introduced myself as a ranger; I didn't really volunteer too much personal information.

—◆—

"I have called us all together today because a team of my scouts has discovered a new cave on a small island in the Haze Cove near Ferrum Mons," the young King began, "This cave is yet unexplored by even the dwarven race, isn't that correct Master Balt?" The ruler asked.

"Aye, M'lord, t'is," Balt agreed, "Me own people 'ave just 'eared of th' cave when that scout'n team came an' took their leave-n-rest in me 'ome town o' Dewarg." The dwarf paused for effect, "Musta been that last quake what shook th' ope'nin' loose."

The King continued, "You each have been chosen by skill and are each known by at least one other present as well," he said as he gestured to the knight, wizard and priest.

The rogue, fighter and I looked at each other and the others, confused.

"Which of ye' knows meself, eh?" Balt challenged.

The halfling priest smiled and raised his chubby little hand, wiggling his plump fingers. "I have gnomish friends in and near Dewarg," Fost stated, "It was *they that* recommended you as the best known fighter in the realm."

It was strange to see a dwarf stricken silent, but to see one blush as well was utterly jaw dropping, so I gathered the statement to be the truth.

Meeka suddenly spoke up and pointed at Loher, "You were the *obvious* choice for our rogue...or thief, if you'll excuse the term.

"Elaborate please," The elven maiden asked sharply, a bit confused.

"I, myself, once tried to catch you, after you stole a ring of mine," the wizard explained, "I'm sure you know by now it was nothing but a trinket and it proved to be worthless to you," she laughed. "But, you had managed to easily evade even my most powerful of magical traps. I stood impressed."

It was then Loher's turn to blush.

I found it all quite intriguing.

"It appears that it must be you, good Sir Knight, that knows me," I guessed, "Yet I am unsure how."

"Correct!" The knight mused, "I shall tell you how." The knight smiled and shifted into a more comfortable position in his chair and then began, "I was just a young boy at the time; I think perhaps I was the age of four. I had wandered from my family while we were on a picnic outing on the shores of Loch Wepan, near the very edge of the Seolfer Wudu. Days had gone by and sadly, my parents had to give up the search to find me. I wandered around for those days, lost among those enchanted trees, looking for my way out, when finally one day you happened to find me."

I smiled a bit also and relaxed back into my chair, "I remember now," I agreed and sat and looked at the knight in awe, "That was *you?*" I reflected. "That was before I could successfully speak the common tongue," I laughed.

"And well before I could speak *a word* of Elven," the knight continued.

"Communication between the two of you must have been *disastrous!*" Brother Fost quipped.

The knight nodded, and then added, "You managed to track down my family, *all the way back* to my home in Herostun and return me safely and anonymously. Yet somehow I remembered throughout all of these years." Sir Quinn's voice trailed off with his thoughts as a vast distant look overtook his eyes momentarily.

"Luck or fate?" I wondered out loud.

"Perhaps a bit of both," the young King stated. "My friends, you all have a grand quest of epic proportions awaiting you on the morrow. Allow me to show you each to your rooms where you may rest and begin fresh and anew in the morning." The young King stood and the rest of us respectfully followed suit.

The King led us down a long hall and as we walked, I couldn't help but think of how strange this all seemed.

I had never met a King, or anyone else of any importance before and the lack of formalities struck me as odd.

The King had asked us not to embellish though, so who was I to blatantly disobey him?

'*Still,*' I thought, '*it just doesn't seem right.*'

One by one, we were shown to our respective rooms to retire for the night.

My room was huge and was of the same gold and white marble.

This room, however, was trimmed in a lavish and exotic dark hardwood.

A thick cream colored rug, perhaps the skin of a yak, lay in the center of the floor and a large natural fieldstone fireplace was mounted snug on the outside wall with two swords crossed behind a coat-of-arms that hung above it.

Large, rich tapestries hung on each wall, depicting battle scenes of old.

The bed, a four post, sat safely but comfortably near the fireplace.

As I lay in the bed, I stared at the fire and slowly dozed off.

I slept.

CHAPTER TWO

BENEVOLENCE

After a good night's sleep and a hearty breakfast of fresh eggs, ham, milk and freshly baked bread, we received some last minute instructions, a badge of the royal crest to wear on our tunics as identification, some funds and some useful provisions; the six of us set out on our way.

It must have just seemed so natural that as we rode on, I, as the ranger and scout, took the lead, joined by our royal escort Sir Quinn.

The dwarven fighter, Balt took up the rear in case we were attacked from behind, while the rest of the party rode along in the middle, randomly switching positions.

We traveled in silence for quite some time until Brother Fost, the halfling, spoke up and broke the still, "Straight off the cuff," the priest began, "I am not ashamed to admit that I will probably be useless in a battle. But rest assured I will not hesitate to heal your wounds and cure your aliments for you as you receive them."

"Take ease, my plump friend," Loher said with a laugh in her words, "you save *my* skin, and *I* will save *yours.*"

"I'll not see any harm come to ye, Priest," Balt added, "So long as ye can cook as well."

"Well, *there's* a *true* dwarf!" The knight bellowed in laughter from up ahead, "Always thinking with his belly!"

"I can cook very well, good dwarf," Fost chuckled, "how do you think all of *this* got here?" He mused as he rubbed his own pudgy tummy.

"I think you may have yourselves a deal," I laughed.

Meeka expressed her agreement by smiling and tousling the halfling priest's hair.

Fost blushed faintly.

We continued on in silence once more, enjoying the 'clipity-clop' of the horses' hooves on the dry, packed dirt path.

The mote-like lake that separated the regal island from the mainland began to show in the not-so-distant foreground, a sign that read: *"North Port Royale"* was just ahead.

A small wooden shack stood next to the long wooden dock that stretched out into the water.

I was very surprised to see a merman sitting at the end of the dock, eating a large fish.

He smiled at me, waved and slid back into the water without even the slightest of splashes.

Two other human men stood talking near the boat, a large, semi-covered ferry.

One of the men was the portman, the other, the ferryman.

The sun glinted, blinding, from the bright blue waves that lapped lazily at the legs of the dock and made the boat lightly bump along its side.

It was a crisp, yet warm spring morning.

Seagulls soared in the clear blue sky, some landing on the shoreline, upsetting the swans, geese and ducks that napped at the water's edge.

The portman looked up and saw our approach.

He excused himself from his conversation with the ferryman and strode toward us, "Do you require passage to the mainland, my friends?" He asked with a low bow.

His bow dipped lower as he noticed the royal badges we wore.

"We do," Sir Quinn stated as the portman rose from his bow.

The portman motioned toward the boat with an exaggerated gesture and the ferryman saluted with a half bow.

"What is the fee?" I asked as I reached for my purse.

"For a royal party such as yourselves? Free, of course!" The portman announced proudly.

"Nonsense," Sir Quinn argued as he reached for his own purse.

"I *insist,* good Sir Knight," The portman protested, "and I will hear not another word about it!" He led us aboard the ferry.

Just to be sure, or perhaps to taunt him, Balt held up a few gold coins to the portman, but the portman still refused and waved them off as if they were annoying flies.

On the boat, the ride to the mainland didn't take as long as it did the night before.

As we were exiting the ferry, I left a small purse on the ferryman's desk.

On the mainland, we could finally, yet barely see the snowy peaks of the mountains, some of which made up the dwarven homeland of Ferrum Mons.

The grey mountains looked like some great maw like a giant ancient beast had taken a large bite out of the bright blue sky.

Snow caps dotted the mountainous peaks in an almost hypnotizing way that made most of us just stop and stare for a moment.

Balt and Fost, being from this part of the realm, were completely unaffected by the view, so they roared out with laughter at our reactions to the glorious sights.

Down in the flat lowlands where we were standing, the wind was forming rolling green waves in the tall grass for almost as far as the eye could see.

A dark hard packed dirt path cut through like a long fat snake.

The longer we rode, the larger the mountains seemed to grow.

As we continued our trek, we sang songs and told stories and myths of olden days to pass the time.

Nearing a large copse of trees that severely darkened the path from the bright sun, I continued the tale I had started a moment before...

"...There are evil creatures that would rather hide in the shadows and cut you down than be seen and fight a fair fight. Damn evil creatures, like my dark cousins, the Drow; the dark elves. Goblins, hobgoblins, giants, bugbears, orcs, and trolls, just to name a few. They can be found in any given spot here in the wilds of Beornan Heafod. Back in the days of olde, going back well more than twenty generations of men, large battles were fought between armies of good and evil. Armies of beasts battled armies of elves, dwarves and man. On and on the battles raged, year after year, good and evil clashed in bloody feuds until one day, a large battalion of dragons of every color and every type, good ones, evil ones, even the neutral ones, formed together under one dragon king and *rose up!* They laid waste to this land, destroying almost all that lived. Those that survived, good and evil alike, scattered to the four winds to hide. Many years later, *life* began to rise up from what was once just ash; *life* has returned to the land that the dragons have named *Beornan Heafod*, which in the olde language means: Burning Head," I paused for effect. "The dragons lay in rest now and nearly centuries later; the armies of evil and darkness are building up once again. We best be wary."

The path we traveled went off to the north east, gradually cutting gently more to the north.

The mountain range grew larger up ahead and to the east.

My home in the enchanted Seolfer Wudu lay off to the very distant south.

I imagine my story had a bit of an impact and gave my companions something to think about, because we rode along in a quieter silence than normal, and I also noticed that everyone looked a little more alert.

Finally, after what seemed like hours, Meeka broke the silence and inquired, "Do you think we will meet any creatures in the cave we are going to?" Her words jarred me away from my own thoughts.

"Aye, Lass," Balt acknowledged, "I'll na' be a bit surprised if we meet up wi' quite a few rotten beasties!" The dwarf sounded slightly excited.

"Rotten?" She asked, "Do you mean... undead?"

"Could," Balt answered, "But that's na' zactly what I was meanin'."

Brother Fost piped up at that moment and proclaimed, "The undead is where my usefulness comes into play!" The halfling reined his pony closer, "We priests have the ability to destroy the undead quite quickly, easily and effectively." He smiled.

"What *else* do you think will be in there?" The wizard calmly asked.

"I guess we will all find *that* out when the time comes," Sir Quinn answered.

Balt grunted out a quick laugh, and then we all fell back into silent thought once again.

The twisting path led us through a grove of dense trees that seemed to loom over us like a group of old maids hovering over a newborn infant.

The foliage tunnel grew darker the deeper we ventured in.

Cautiously, we wove our way through the trees.

The wind whipped through the narrow tunnel and down the twisting path making a hollow howling moan, like a large lonely wolf.

I saw the makings of fear on the faces of a few of my companions; I'll not mention their names out of respect.

Sir Quinn must have noticed their fear as well, because he slowed his horse down and allowed the group to tighten up a bit.

The fearful looks eroded in time and after a while, we emerged safely on the other side of the trees.

Just ahead, a small town could be seen and the sign ahead read: *'Now Entering Steorra.'*

The mountains loomed higher, now more to our east.

The path twisted and turned along.

All of a sudden, we noticed an alarming amount of smoke rising from the town and the closer we got, the better we could hear the tolling of the town's alarm bell and the angry and frightened shouts of the townsfolk.

Concerned, we all rode at full gallop toward the burning town.

As we entered, we saw that some of the houses and storefronts were set ablaze.

The townsfolk rushed around with pails of water trying futilely to put the smoking blaze out.

Quickly scanning the area, Balt and I discovered a group of goblins throwing torches onto a house, while another group attacked a group of men.

"I'll stay with the mounts!" Brother Fost yelled.

Without hesitation, Balt, Quinn and I dismounted and engaged the enemy.

Swinging my sword in mid-sprint, I felled my first two goblins, taking each by complete surprise.

I cut the first one down with one stroke, but the second one took a slice and a stab.

Balt's Great Axe made short work of another.

I lost sight of my companions just after I observed Meeka extinguish a great deal of the flames with a '*water cone' spell,* which created a thick wall of rolling smoke and steam.

We smiled at each other as we became lost in the thickening cloud.

Moments later, Sir Quinn emerged from within the hazy murk with a blood covered blade, "Mark down two for me!" The knight announced proudly, and then disappeared back into the gloom.

I took a deep breath and dove in myself.

It was so difficult to see in so much blur, so I picked a direction and went forward in a straight line until I witnessed a man get cut down by an orc warrior.

Before I could properly react, the orc saw me and swung at me wildly, connecting his rusty unkempt blade with my left shoulder; a fine spray of my blood erupted causing slight pain.

I thrust my sword at him and buried the blade deep into his belly.

I then gave the blade a good twist and a violent yank hard to the left so my blade would cut through and become free.

The orc warrior looked directly at me with wide eyes.

I could see the life slowly drain away from them as a look of sick pain washed over his piglike features.

He dropped to his knees and fell over, dead.

I once again became aware of the sounds of battle; steel against steel rang out through the smoke, mixed with the agonizing screams of pain and shouts of frustration and anger.

An arrow swiftly zipped closely past my head, and thudded into something firm, yet wet behind me.

I quickly turned to see a hobgoblin standing right there behind me with his sword raised as if to slice me in two.

An arrow abruptly replaced his left eye.

The monster fell dead at my feet as I heard Loher call out, "Thank me later!" from across the way.

I could feel the oozing of my blood as it made its way down my arm under my armor from my throbbing shoulder to my wrist.

The smoke was twisting into tiny tornados as it began to clear; my search for the attackers continued.

I moved closer toward the sounds of battle; flames licked at me from my right, so I strafed off to the left and continued to surge my way forward.

Up ahead, I could see the blade of Balt's Great Axe slice cleanly through a goblin, cleaving the creature into equal halves at the dwarf's feet.

Balt roared in victory!

"I see ye got yerself a wee boo-boo there," he snorted as he slapped my wounded left shoulder.

I winced in pain as he roared out with even more laughter.

An orc soldier swiftly appeared through the smoke, directly behind Balt, and without even thinking; I lunged over the dwarf's shoulder and beheaded the foe.

Balt was taken by surprise by my quick reflexes.

He gleamed with pride and once again roared out with hearty laughter.

I erupted with laughter as well, then we noticed that the smog had lifted enough to see that the townspeople had rounded up the rest of the vile creatures that had attacked their town, and rustled them up into an empty barn, killing them one by one; The people cheered with each and every kill.

We quietly gathered our party together and met Brother Fost and our mounts by the gates.

We mounted and departed with no words.

⸺◆⸺

Further down the path, as the sun began to set, we found a substantially sized grove of trees and set up our camp.

As we set up camp, Brother Fost seemed gleeful and pranced around as happy as can be.

"Now *my* duty begins!" He excitedly announced and quickly began building a campfire.

Meeka tended to our mounts, Loher took her bow and went hunting for our supper, and Balt went about cleaning and sharpening our weapons, while Sir Quinn and I checked the perimeter and took watch.

A half an hour later, Loher returned to the camp with a dozen fat rabbits, the arrows still jutting from the cooling limp bodies, and handed them to Brother Fost.

The halfling priest made quick work of skinning, cleaning and cooking them on spits over the fire.

As the food slowly cooked, the priest turned to me and said, "Now, let's take a look at that shoulder of yours."

I removed my armor, and as I did, Balt snatched it up quickly and began repairs on it.

"This is not so bad," the priest mumbled at the wound, "I have seen far worse," he said as he gingerly poked his thumb at the slice.

I drew a sharp breath through gritted teeth, "Says you," I groaned, then I heard a slight giggle from somewhere behind me.

The halfling priest of Onh began to chant some holy words and wave his hands over my wounded shoulder.

It began to itch horribly, then before my very own eyes; the slice in my shoulder closed up and started to heal.

The pain and itching quickly subsided and eventually went away entirely.

My newly mended armor was sitting at my side by the time Brother Fost was done healing my wound.

My armor actually fit better once I got it back on and I gave Balt a nod of thanks, as well as one to Brother Fost.

As Brother Fost tended to the food, I took a stroll around the camp.

I noticed Balt eyeing up the cooking rabbits like an owl would eye up a field mouse.

The sight of those rabbits made my mind drift away to that odd race I had witnessed on the trail the day before.

A slight pattering scamper in the brush to my right stirred me out of my dreamlike state.

I looked around using my ranger skills, but saw nothing.

As the sun set on our party, nestled in our meager camp in the woods, our campfire cast strange shadows around us all.

The wind blew the dead leaves and clouds of dust around in those familiar tight little tornados, stirring up glowing embers from the fire, making them dance like tiny orange stars that sank too close to the ground to survive.

Sir Quinn set two fresh logs on the fire, as Brother Fost handed out the food.

We all ate our fill as we each told stories from our varied pasts, but *this time* we tried to keep it light and humorous.

The events of the day had tired us out, and one by one, all but Loher drifted off to sleep.

As I lie there dozing off and gazing at the flickering fire, I *thought* I caught a glimpse of a few small faces in the shadows beyond the flames.

Before I could react, I found that the fire had burned way down and the moon had moved to a later position in the sky.

As I arose, I felt refreshed as if *I had* slept for a few hours as the moon's present position suggested.

I set a few fresh logs on the fire, and then went over to sit by Loher.

"How are you doing?" I asked her softly, as to not wake the others.

"I am faring well, did you have a nice sleep?" she asked.

Confused, I didn't answer.

She studied my face for a while, and then asked, "Are *you* alright?"

"As I was falling asleep," I began, "I was looking into the fire and *I swear* I saw a few small faces in the shadows just beyond the fire," I paused, "The *next* thing I knew, I was sitting here, with you."

We sat in silence, watching the fire and after a short time we shared the sunrise as it began to crest over the horizon.

Loher slowly rose, put her finger to her lips and whispered, "Shhh!! I shall return shortly."

She grabbed up her bow and disappeared silently into the forest.

A few moments later, she returned just as silently, back to the camp carrying several large pheasants, already plucked and gutted.

The party awoke to the delightful smells of the cooking birds.

We all took our fill, then gathered our gear and hid the camp.

"I wonder if the townsfolk in Steorra knew that they had any help." Meeka wondered out loud.

"I agree, I wonder if they even knew we were there." Brother Fost commented.

"I wonder if it should really even matter to any of us." Sir Quinn calmly countered.

"I think it will take some time for most of us to get used to being selfless." I stated out into the open, directly at no one.

My statement drew some understanding looks and nods of agreement.

We rode on in our usual blanket of silence for quite a while as the sun finally fully crested over the horizon and took the chilly bite out of the crisp spring morning air.

<hr>

After a few hours of steady riding and idle chat, we decided to stop and let our mounts have a well-deserved rest.

We had found a place with a small fresh water pond and a tall weeping willow tree that produced enough shade from the now warming sun that sat high in the sky.

We sat there for a while, enjoying dried fruits and meat, as our mounts grazed and drank from the pond.

The air was becoming warmer and more humid.

We noticed the sky had begun to quickly cloud over and grow darker.

"It looks as though we may be in for some rain," I said, as I looked up at the rapidly building clouds.

My companions looked to the sky as well.

Sir Quinn walked up and stood beside me, "How long?" He asked.

I bent down and scooped up some loose, dry dirt and let it run slowly through my relaxed fist like the sands of an hourglass.

The dust floated away and swirled around in the strengthening wind.

"Two hours, perhaps a bit more." I reported.

"It will take a little under an hour to get to Avilyn Harbor," Sir Quinn advised, "Perhaps we should cut our rest stop short and move along now."

I agreed and we rousted the team, telling them of the pending weather.

We were all up and moving in less than ten minutes, even our mounts seemed to have found new energy, as we arrived at the harbor in just over a half hour.

As we approached the harbor, the sky had grown much darker as the clouds overtook the sun.

A sky that was once a bright clear robin's egg blue, had changed to a dark, puffy grey and white blur that looked more like the beard on an ancient wizard's chin.

The unmistakable low rumble of distant thunder was crawling in from the west.

As the wind picked up, old leaves from last year's shed of autumn blew around in their usual tight circles, like invisible whirlpools of air.

We dismounted our horses and stowed them in the harbor's common corral.

As we were heading toward the harbor's dock house door, something flashed bright green on the ground near the roots of a tree, and caught my attention from the corner of my eye.

I paused and looked directly toward it, but there was nothing there.

I shrugged it off and followed my companions to the door of the dock house.

I took one last look over my shoulder at the roots of that tree and saw not one, but a half dozen fairies standing there in a group, looking directly back at me.

I had an overwhelming sense of déjà vu'.

I blinked, and they were gone as if they had never even been there.

"McLaaud," Brother Fost called as he held the door open and waited for me, "are you coming in?" He asked and studied me with curiosity.

I rubbed my eyes and half smiled at the halfling, "Yeah," I began, as I stepped closer to the door, "I just thought I saw—"

I then stopped talking as I saw that he was not listening.

The harbormaster was speaking loudly, "I'm sorry," he said, "Royal business or not, you'll just have to wait until that storm blows over before I let any of my ships or boats set sail!"

"Good Harbormaster, I assure you," Sir Quinn began calmly in a soothing voice, "we are in no position, and better still, we have no desire to argue with your rules."

Relieved, the harbormaster gave a great sigh, smiled and gave thanks.

Balt quietly called us all over to the side of the room, "I know a wee shortcut through th' mountains an' through Ferrum Mons as well," he said, "but we're gonna have ta backtrack a wee bit ta git there. What'ch ye say, Mates?" The dwarf asked with a fire in his eyes.

"How far back?" I asked.

"Just te th' other side o' that waterin' hole," he answered.

———— ◆ ————

After a unanimous vote, we all decided that perhaps it *would* be best if we backtracked to the watering hole we camped at as the storm began to creep in, assuming the trek would take less than the hour we originally figured we had before the worst of the storm would hit.

Brother Fost led the way out to the harbor's common corral. I volunteered to take up the rear. (So I could secretly look to see if those fairies were still there by the roots of that old tree... they were not.)

I quickly took a good look around to assess the situation when out of the blue—

"It has become quite apparent that you have either come across something of great interest, or you've become distracted," Brother Fost said and startled me as he handed me the reigns of my horse.

"Thank you for fetching my horse, Brother," I muttered as I mounted.

The halfling gave me a questioning look, but I just shook it off and urged Stahvee off into a trot toward the watering hole.

I thought it better not to speak out my thoughts of the fairies yet, not until I had evident proof of them.

A wise man once said: "It is better to remain silent and be thought a fool, than to speak unwisely and remove all doubt." I decided to wait.

It was almost as dark as night, as the storm clouds had all but gobbled up the midday sun.

We had to backtrack to the south.

Off to our right, we could see even darker clouds rolling in, briefly illuminated by violent lightning, viciously spider webbing across the turbulent sky.

Moments later, a loud cracking bash of thunder would follow each flash and rumble its echo into decay.

Our mounts would quicken their pace with each splintering crash.

Violent gusts of driving wind whipped through us, almost knocking poor Brother Fost from his pony, which was almost being lifted from the ground.

The pony screamed out in horror which startled the rest of our mounts.

"Be calm, my friend, be calm," I cooed, lightly stroking Stahvee's neck and shoulders. "It's just the storm." This seemed to calm him down, calming the rest of the animals down in turn.

Just ahead, I pointed out the familiar willow tree that was now bending against the power of the heavy wind.

"We be gettin' close now, Mates!" Balt called out as we passed by the willow and pond, "Head far ta mountains, I'll be takin' ta lead!" The dwarf quickened his pace with Brother Fost right on his heels.

Sir Quinn and I slowed down enough to let the women into the center of the group and then we took up the rear.

"I really hope he knows what he's doing!" The knight shouted to me over the wind.

"I'm sure he does!" I yelled back, "These mountains are his home; I think we should trust him!"

"We have absolutely no reason *not* to trust him!" Sir Quinn yelled back, with a wide smile.

As we finally reached the beginning of the mountains, Balt slowed his pace, "Be keepin' yor eyes open far a large red rock tat seems ta not belong tere," he called out, "An' be lettin' me know when ye found it!"

We all spread out and methodically searched for the red rock he spoke of.

I used my infrared elven-sight as I assumed Loher did as well.

Brother Fost and the wizard, Meeka used their *'light' spells* and Balt looked around with his apparent fuzzy memory.

Sir Quinn and I kept a look-out for foes.

Wind violently whipped around us as the storm blew in closer.

"I thought you knew where this passage was!" Sir Quinn called out to Balt, impatiently.

"Keep yor damn tunic on, Knight!" The dwarf grumbled, "S'been *ages* since I've hadda use it."

"Define '*ages.*'" Sir Quinn snapped back.

"Longer'n *ye've* been alive, ya—"Balt began...

But Meeka cut him off with...   "I think I found it Balt!"

"Hold yor position, Lass!" The dwarf shouted out into the air as he shot the knight a look, "I'll be right wit'cha!" The dwarf quickly and nimbly navigated the rocky terrain and raced to catch up with the wizard.

As the dwarf reached the wizard, a large toothy smile emerged upon the scarred chipped toothed face, "Very *good* girl!" The dwarf complimented, but it sounded more like, "Verra guid gieril!" because of his thick dwarven accent. "Ye found it!"

The dwarf then reached into his pouch on his belt and produced a small ornately carved flutelike instrument, "We dwarves be full've all sorts o' surprises!" he said, and then played a few curious notes.

As if on cue, two things began to happen at once.

The first was a low rumbling sound that seemed to grind forth from deep within the ground, a large puff of dank chalky dust burst out from a crack that had formed in the rock and continues up the face of the mountain.

The second was that the wind had calmed down just enough for fat raindrops, some the size of chicken eggs, some larger, to fall straight down with such force that they almost hurt when they hit bare flesh.

The fresh clean smell of rain on dry stone filled the warm spring air.

The rumbling and grinding of the opening crack in the rock face continued until the opening became a passage large enough for two large horses to pass through, side by side.

The wind started back up, even stronger than before, and the fat raindrops came down in sheets.

Two gnomes abruptly appeared from within the passage; Balt stepped forward and spoke to them in an odd, yet strangely familiar tongue.

Balt then turned and quickly ushered us into the secret passage and down into a different tunnel.

The gnomes led us hastily, single file, over a narrow, rickety rope bridge as the secret crack passage closed up behind us.

Upon reaching the other side of the bridge, we found ourselves in a large dimly lit cavern occupied by other dwarves, gnomes and harmless large eyed humanoid creatures that stood less than a foot tall, called Pech.

These hard working subterranean creatures were rarely, if ever, found above ground.

The sunlight, even in small amounts, painfully hurt their large eyes.

None of us, besides Balt and perhaps Brother Fost, had seen such a thing ever before in our lives.

None of the miners from either race paid any apparent attention to us as we quickly passed through.

The dimly lit cavern sparkled with various precious metals and gems, which were naturally encrusted within the walls, floor and ceiling.

The miners worked diligently, humming and chanting as they picked, dug and scooped away.

Large piles of electrum, gold, silver, copper and various precious stones lay littered upon the floor of the cavern.

As if we were intruding on some well-kept secret (which we were,) we were quickly ushered through yet another passageway that led to places already mined and cleaned out of materials.

Before we were led away too far, I looked back and saw that the rope bridge we crossed was gone with no trace of it anywhere.

Through all this, the wind had picked up even more as a violent storm was beating mercilessly upon the mountains above.

We all walked along in silent awe as we moved through the caverns, wondering if the new cave we were ordered to explore would be at all like this.

The sounds of shovels and pick axes became faint as we moved deeper and further into the mountain.

The storm became increasingly violent outside as the outer rim of the storm broke through the peaks and valleys of the mountains above our heads.

The wind outside picked up even more speed as it whipped through the narrow channels and paths.

Inside, the passageways twisted, turned and branched out in virtually every direction wherever the veins of precious material led.

It was a maze down there that only the miners knew the true way through and just as we thought the tour was over, the tunnel would open up into yet another larger cavernous room.

"Got us a guid storm a brewin' up out there Mates!" Balt quipped. "I ain't hear'ed one ta likes o' this fer a hunnerd, a hunnerd fifty'r more years!" His eyes were wild and wide with excitement.

"How far under the surface do you think we are, Master Dwarf?" Sir Quinn asked, his voice barely heard above the screaming wind outside.

"Ta thinnest parts would be b'tween ta peaks an' would be averagin' 'bout three hunnerd foot thick," Balt answered.

We continued on through the mountains and after a few more twists and turns, the familiar aroma of cooking meats and the sounds of commerce began to surround us.

We emerged through a hidden narrow passage just barely large enough to squeeze our largest horse through, to see a bustling city center.

"Ladies an' gents," Balt began with a gesturing sweep of his hand, "Welcome ta Dewarg, Capital of ta Ferrum Mons, homeland of ta dwarven race."

⸻◆⸻

Dewarg

The subterranean cavernous town that made up the only part of the Ferrum Mons that was publicly accessible.

Quite like Larix was within the Seolfer Wudu, homeland of the elven race, and the much, much more private, yet still publicly accessible Hydan Seir, capital of Leah, homeland of the halfling race.

From where we stood, the town of Dewarg opened up into a flickering, yet dimly lit cavern with a very wide pillar formed directly in the center of the town proper, creating a wide circular round-a-bout type passage that ran around and then back into its self like a large snake wrapped around and swallowed its own tail.

Many large shallow cut-outs were carved into the walls of the circular passage creating shoppes and guilds.

Among these shoppes were weaponries, armories, tool shoppes, even food eateries.

Dozens of patrons moved about from shoppe to shoppe.

Among the dwarves that made up over half of the percentage of patrons, there were gnomes, halflings, a few elves and even some men.

Balt then pointed to the passage leading back to the outside world and we could still hear the storm raging out there, calming a bit, but still very strong.

"I cannot decide which be louder, Mates," Balt chuckled patting his belly, "Ta rumblin' o' me tummy er ta thunder in ta sky."

We all laughed, then Balt pointed out a tavern, properly called the 'Ale House.'

We decided perhaps a nice leisurely meal and some drinks would do fine while we waited out the storm a bit longer.

The 'Ale House' was set up quite a bit like 'The Broken Blade' was in the royal city of Salvus Hus.

The only difference was it was missing the table in the southeast corner by the door.

We took our usual northwestern corner table by the fireplace and ordered our meals and drinks.

As we waited, we chatted amongst ourselves and I took a good look around at our surroundings.

Of the thirty-seven possible seats, eighteen were taken (twenty-four including our party of six.)

Of those eighteen, fourteen were dwarves which was not uncommon in Dewarg, and of the four remaining, scattered within, one was a human female, one was a gnomish male and in the last two seats, together sat a pair of elves. (Lovers perhaps?)

The elves sat at the southwestern corner table; the human female sat at the most northern stool at the bar and with an empty stool between them, to the south sat the gnome. (I was not sure if they were together, I assumed not.)

Sitting at the two most southern stools at the bar, were an obvious pair of dwarven lovers, which was odd, because public displays of affection between dwarves was almost unheard of.

The remaining twelve dwarves took up the two tables in the center of the room; their tables were pushed together as this was a large party celebrating the death of a loved one.

After some diplomatic questioning from Balt, it was discovered that the deceased was no one Balt had known, but the knowledge had compelled him to relay his condolences to the survivors.

The elven lovers now seemed to pay more attention to us than they did to each other, as they unsuccessfully tried to hide their interest.

Balt returned to our table with a pained look deep within his eyes, as our food and drink was being served.

As we ate, we unanimously decided that it was just too crowded and too risky to openly discuss our mission, especially because the elven lovers at the nearest table were still obviously eyeing us suspiciously.

Instead, we decided to tell amusing stories, jokes and riddles.

Within that time, the storm outside had calmed enough that I, for one, could no longer hear it from within our subterranean shelter.

We leisurely took our time eating and visiting to ensure the worst of the storm had passed; two hours had gone by, and the elven lovers were still quite curiously (yet still trying to look casual) paying close attention to us.

Meeka seemed not to notice them, "That was quite a storm!" She said with a relieved look upon her youthful face.

"I wonder if it's over," Brother Fost added.

"Not quite yet," Loher announced softly, "I can still hear it out there."

If I listened intently, I could still barely hear the low rumble of distant thunder with my half-elven ears, so I could only imagine what the full blooded elf, Loher was hearing.

We continued to enjoy ourselves, and after another hour or so, Loher had informed us that the storm had all but completely passed, so as the barmaid came to refill our drinks, we paid our bill and left the tavern.

As we exited the cave, the midday sun, now visible, was lower in the sky and I estimated that we had another two full hours of good, strong sunlight before the sun would decide to duck out on us and retire for the night.

The naturally walled outskirts of Dewarg were dotted with both natural and dwarven carved caves that made up the not-so-crude homes of the dwarves and some gnomes.

Paths through the mountains led in all different directions, but a sign that read: '*TO HARBOR*' pointed to a path leading northeast.

"If we want to get to the new cave, I suggest we go see the harbormaster." I said, pointing at the sign.

My companions agreed, so we began to walk down the hill toward the sea.

The path led steeply down the mountain, just steep enough that we had to walk our mounts safely behind us.

The downward path twisted and turned so much, we had to pay constant attention to avoid danger, while Balt and Brother Fost seemed to easily navigate down the steep and narrow terrain.

Awesome and beautiful hues of oranges, pinks and purples streaked across the clouds dissipating in the sky, creating a natural painting of glorious color.

By the time we had reached the bottom at the harbor, the sun had completely set and the sky was wide and clear, brandishing bright, twinkling stars and a brilliant full moon of the palest color of cream.

Brother Fost was gently humming in a low voice.

We stowed our mounts in the harbor's common corral under the authority of the King, spoke to the harbormaster of our intentions, then boarded the ship called *The Scorpion* with a full crew, and set sail for the new cave.

The Scorpion looked unlike any other ship we had ever seen before, for it looked like a giant golden scorpion set atop the lower decks of a large wooden ship.

Aboard *The Scorpion,* Sir Quinn produced a map of The Haze, the area of Beornan Heafod where the islands sat, and shared it with *The Scorpion*'s captain, "Do you know of this island, Captain?" He asked, pointing at the map.

"Me been sailin' deese wa'ters since me was just a boi, Mon," said the captain, an odd young human man whose skin tone was a bit darker than that of the Drow elves.

His hair was thick and long, and resembled braided rope.

The members of the crew looked just the same.

"This is a *new* cave we seek." The knight offered.

"Diss I know, Mon," The captain said slyly, "an' I can teal ya now dat de cave dat ya seeks is not so farawee." ("...is not so far away.")

The Scorpion silently navigated through the waters of The Haze, the area of the realm where the tiny lifeless islands were found.

The captain called out orders to his crew, occasionally warning them to be careful of the submerged rocks below the water's surface.

A crewman leaned way over The Scorpion's bow, verbally guiding the helmsman through the many unseen rocks.

The Scorpion lightly bounced off of rocks from time to time, but with little to no damage done to the ship.

It was slow going for a while as The Scorpion tip-toed along toward the island cave.

Eventually, a small dock reached out to the ship from an island to the left.

The island itself was just a cropping of mountains that looked as if they were just floating motionlessly in the sea.

My heart sunk as I noticed cave openings all over the faces of the mountains on this island.

I could see a mutual expression upon the face of my knighted companion, an expression of slight panic and disappointment that the captain had led us to the wrong island.

As if he had read our minds, the captain spoke up, "Thems not de caves dat'cha be lookin' for, Mon." He was smiling and pointing at the island. "I tolds ya I be knowin what'cha be meanin'. No worries, ja?" The captain said, and then laughed.

Sir Quinn looked, and then laughed as well.

A relieved look suddenly washed across Sir Quinn's face, making my stress melt away too.

We swung swiftly around another chain of islands, then the captain announced, "De'ar ja go, bruddahs an' sistahs," the ship and his finger both pointed dead toward an island with a single raw cave opening on top of a mountain, "Unfa'rtunately, me cant's get'cha no closer den dis."

The wizard, Meeka, abruptly spoke up, "That will not be a problem," she said, "Gather around me, my friends, whoever's going ashore."

We all gathered around the red headed wizard as she told the captain and crew to take a few steps back.

Meeka closed her eyes and raised her hands in the air as she began to chant some mysterious words in some ancient tongue.

The air around us became thick, as if with a slight electrical charge.

Gradually, that familiar pink misty fog that we had seen in the throne room back at the castle in the Royal city of Salvus Hus appeared around us.

Our group of adventurous companions began to tighten up and draw closer to each other, then...

POP!

The pink misty fog began to clear and we found ourselves standing on the shoreline of the island, looking out at The Scorpion, pink misty fog was clearing from the deck where we all once stood as well.

The captain called to us from the deck of the ship, "I'll be back in de mornin' wit some dockin' supplies an' a smaller boat!"

The Scorpion then set sail for the harbor.

"Well," Balt said as he dug a few torches from his pack, "what're we waitn' fer?" The dwarf lit a few of the torches and passed them out.

Slowly we ascended to the mouth of the cave, steadily climbing; within the hour, one by one, I, the ranger, in the lead, closely followed by the knight, we entered the new cave.

Brother Fost followed Sir Quinn, then the wizard and the rogue, while the dwarven fighter took up the rear.

Chapter Three
HOLLOW

I was very surprised to notice, as I first entered the narrow passage, that we may not really be the first to enter this new cave.

"Balt, Sir Quinn," I hissed behind me, "Hold!"

The team abruptly stopped at my command and Sir Quinn made his way closer to talk to me.

"What did you find, McLaaud?" The knight asked as he finally arrived at my position.

"Tracks," I whispered my answer back, "We're not alone. There are tracks of some kind on the archway, but none on the floor."

My companions looked at me with confused, questioning looks across their faces.

"I'm not entirely sure what it is," I said, "but it's definitely *not* humanoid."

Their looks became even more confused and almost frightened.

"What do the tracks look like?" Sir Quinn quietly asked.

"It's difficult to tell," I began, "here, let me show you." I said and pointed out the strange tracks on the archway. "As far as I can tell, these markings look as though they were made by bats, which in itself are not so uncommon within a cave such as this, but these particular markings are **huge!**" I paused for a moment to gauge each of their reactions, Balt and Sir Quinn looked both excited and interested; Loher simply looked attentive but not very thrilled, while Brother Fost and Meeka showed signs of being worried and perhaps a bit afraid.

I continued, "The only thing that makes me believe that it may not be bats is the lack of guano."

"Guano?" Meeka asked.

"Waste," I answered, "droppings, p—"

"I get it!" She cut me off, disgusted.

"So, let me get this straight," the knight started, "the tracks look like they might be left by giant bats, but you're not absolutely sure?"

"Correct," I answered, "I'm unsure because of the lack of –"

"DON'T say it!" Meeka hissed quickly cutting me off again.

"So what do we do now?" Brother Fost whispered with a slight tremble in his breath.

"I say we press on bravely ahead, Mates," Balt huffed and playfully nudged the Halfling Priest.

"We really have no other choice," I agreed with a slight smile.

"I have a bad feeling about this," Meeka muttered under her breath as the party continued to follow me into the dimly lit cave.

"I can hear the sound of rushing water ahead, McLaaud," Loher quietly announced, "but it sounds as if it's far away and seemingly below us somehow."

"I can't hear anything," Sir Quinn said in an undoubting manner.

"Nor meself, Mate," Balt quietly agreed.

I decided to stay quiet although after the fact that Loher had pointed out the sound, I too could faintly hear it.

The passage we followed opened up into a wide cavernous chasm.

Our path turned into a narrow ledge on the side of a wall with a sheer straight drop down to our right that promised instant death if one would happen to slip and fall.

The wall was on our left and it curved around and seemed to disappear from sight off to the further left ahead of us, then reappeared again as it curved around to the right to create the walls that encompassed us as a room.

I looked down to my right, down the sheer deadly drop to see the ground below.

It was there, as was the reason for the faint rushing water sound as there was what looked to us from this height, a small trickling stream, but in all truth and reality, it was a very wide and violently tormenting white watered river. (A class five at the very least!)

In order to formerly gauge the distance from us to the river, Brother Fost decided to drop a coin and count the time it took until we heard it hit the bottom...

... (Until we heard it hit the bottom...)

... (Ummm...Hit Bottom???)

We never heard a thing besides the low rushing sound of the river below.

Way, way down below.

We cautiously continued down, along the ledge as it curved to the left around the bend then disappeared into a hole in the wall.

Darkness.

As we slowly, cautiously entered the tunnel, our torches illuminated the archway and floor around us.

I searched for tracks but came up empty.

"No tracks," I whispered back.

This information helped relax the more nervous half of my crew (a bit.)

As we continued down into the tunnel, it sharply forked off to the left, again into the wall.

The original tunnel continued sloping downward in the same forward direction we were already headed.

I stopped at the fork to examine the left tunnel...

About twenty feet down, I noticed some odd webbed footprints in the deep dust on the floor.

I quickly made my way back to the party to report what I had discovered.

"There are some tracks on the floor in there that come to the end of the tunnel, then abruptly turn around and go back in," I reported.

"Can you tell what kind of tracks they are?" Sir Quinn asked, with a raise in his voice.

"Humanoid," I began, "with clawed, webbed toes, possibly reptilian."

After a moment of thought, the knight reflected, "It seems as though we have a few choices." The knight paused and looked at each of us, as if to gain our attention, "One, we can explore this tunnel; two, we can continue down the ledge, or; three, we can split up into two teams and explore both then meet back here shortly."

"We should put it to a vote," Brother Fost suggested.

My companions and I looked around from face to face, searching each other for some sort of answer.

Swiftly, Brother Fost violently shoved me out of the way as the blade of a sword sliced the air between us and rang out sharply as it struck the stone floor.

I quickly turned to look directly into the cold eyes of a creature that looked to be half human and half lizard.

It stood about five and a half feet tall, weighing a muscular 200 pounds with dark green and golden brown scales.

Its face, hands, feet and tail resembled that of an iguana.

It was wearing strapped leather armor and wielded a crude sword.

The creature suddenly hissed at me and swung around, smashing me with his tail and quickly bolted back down the tunnel.

I was knocked off my feet and into a wall, and I noticed that Balt and Sir Quinn gave chase to the creature.

"Are you in need of healing?" Brother Fost asked as he knelt beside me concerned.

"No," I answered as Loher helped me to my feet, "But I do owe you both a word of thanks for saving my skin. You just now," I said to the priest, then turned to Loher, "and you in Steorra."

Loher just blinked in understanding at me, and then with a gleam in her eyes, she took off running down the tunnel after our friends.

The priest, the wizard and I followed shortly after.

As we made our way through the tunnel, we had to jump over the corpse of the creature we just encountered.

Yet shouts and the sounds of fighting floated to our ears from just ahead.

A chamber opened widely from the tunnel, brightly lit by torch light.

There was no exit.

A dozen or more of the lizard-like creatures surrounded Balt and Sir Quinn, as the dwarf cut one down with his Great Axe and the knight herded the rest into a loose group.

Loher let loose with an arrow that thwipped into a scaly green face, dropping the creature instantly as I dove into another.

My sword slashed through its neck and its head lolled off its shoulders, eyes still blinking trying to focus.

Blood cast off in a large gouting spurt.

Crimson streaks of gore oozed to the floor down the walls.

Loher drew back her bow once again and let it fly as Meeka chanted the mystic words of an ancient spell.

The arrow found its mark, burying deep into the lizard's chest, while several small balls of flame soared over our heads, produced magically from the wizard's hands, and smashed into their targets sending scaly flesh to flame.

The room brightened with the growing flames from the burning reptilian bodies. Acrid smoke rose to the ceiling and began to fill the room.

Surprised by the sudden burst of flame, Balt instinctively ducked and tumbled, mistakenly letting the creatures loose from the corner.

One of the creatures hissed as it jumped over Balt and then ran down the tunnel past a stunned Brother Fost.

Shaking the cobwebs from his head, Brother Fost gave chase after the creature, his little legs pumping and churning, trying to keep up with the fleeing lizard.

One of the three remaining creatures took a wild swipe with a sword and connected with Balt's helmed head, as another creature lunged at me.

Balt roared as he swung his Great Axe about and cut the legs out from under his attacker, while I buried my blade into the chest of mine.

"I'm going after Fost!" Sir Quinn called as he ran from the room and disappeared down the tunnel.

Instinctively, I thrust my blade behind me under my left armpit and impaled the last foe in the chest.

The creature dropped in a heap at my heels as blood pooled at my feet.

The room was growing hotter and it was becoming more and more difficult to breathe from the smoke coming from the burning lizard bodies, so my companions and I poured along with the smoke from the room and down the tunnel.

Upon arriving back at the fork, I noticed the knight had the last of the creatures alive and at bay.

"Look what I caught," Brother Fost said proudly, pointing at the lizard.

"You did well, Priest," Loher said as she messed the halfling's hair with her hand.

The sound of rushing water filled the silence between words.

As we heard a low growl behind us, we turned to see Balt with his hands holding his belly.

"To meself, the smell o' that smoke was a wee bit appetizing," he said with a hardy laugh.

I aimed my attention at the creature the knight had at bay.

It stood eyes wide, its hands in a shielding defensive position.

I walked closer to it and put my hand on Sir Quinn's blade so he'd lower it, then asked in a calm, cool voice, "Why did your friend attack me?"

The lizard did not answer.

"Perhaps it doesn't understand you," Loher commented.

She then tried to ask calmly in the Elven language.

No answer.

Balt tried in both the dwarven and gnomish tongues.

No answer to either.

Every language we tried brought no response.

"I would like to search for clues in that room they were in," Loher stated.

"As would I," I agreed.

"I suggest we all go and take him with us, "Sir Quinn said as he coaxed the oversized iguana toward the tunnel.

"Aye," Balt agreed. "Perhaps the sight o' his dead mateys'll get the beastie talkin'!"

"It's worth a try," I said as I started toward the tunnel, Loher hot on my heels.

Meeka quickly ran off ahead, chanting another spell as she disappeared into the tunnel.

After a few minutes, the flickering fire light went dark, and a low steady sizzling noise crept from the tunnel.

Smoke was replaced with a lighter colored steam.

"Illuminare!" Meeka cried after a few minutes more, and then the tunnel erupted with a bright, steady light.

We met her halfway through the tunnel, "I put out the fires and shed some new light on the subject," she giggled, then turned back around and we all entered the room.

Balt took control of the lizard-man and Sir Quinn stood by the mouth of the tunnel.

Loher and I methodically searched the room and corpses, while Brother Fost studied some rune like markings on a wall.

The wizard, Meeka, seemed to pace the room with a blank look upon her beautifully featured face.

To this day, I still don't know what was going through her mind.

After a few moments, as Brother Fost copied down the rune- like markings onto a piece of parchment, Meeka walked over to him and asked, "Can you make any sense of those markings?"

"No, not entirely," the priest answered, as he carefully stuffed the folded up parchment into a deep pocket located inside of his robes, "These symbols seem to be part of some kind of a story... or... well, to be perfectly honest, I don't quite know yet."

He smiled nervously.

The wizard smiled back, giggled and clapped the nervous priest gently on his back in an affectionate manner.

Meanwhile, Loher and I completed our search and discovered nothing but an odd trinket, a small chunk of bone that was ornately carved into a fascinating shape.

The sight of this trinket made the lizard-man stir when he saw it.

"Well, well, well!" Balt exclaimed, "Thare be a reaction!"

Loher brought the trinket closer to the reptile.

It lunged at the elven maiden and tried to grab the object from her hand, but the nimble elf dodged away from his unsuccessful grasp.

"What IS this?" She asked the creature as she held the object in plain view.

The creature just blinked its eyes, mouth clamped shut.

"Well then, perhaps I should just destroy it, hmmm?" She said coyly and raised the bone trinket high above her head, acting as if she meant to forcibly smash it down to the stone surface of the cave's floor.

She brought her hand, holding the bone object, down quickly—

"NO!!!" The lizard-man shrieked in fear as it tore away from the dwarf's grasp and dove to the floor, as if to intercept the object and save it from total destruction.

The object stayed firmly in Loher's hand.

Loher smiled as she quickly moved the bone object away and produced a sharp dagger, which she instantly had to the throat of the creature, now on his back, on the floor.

"It speaks!" Balt mused in surprise.

"Tell me what this is!" Loher demanded; her purple-violet eyes were ablaze.

"It is a holy charm!" The creature hissed out in fear.

Loher looked at the item in her hand, turning it over and examining it completely.

The bone trinket was about six inches long and three inches wide, carved ornately from what might have been perhaps the leg bone of some mid-sized creature.

It resembled some sort of totem.

Loher looked up at me, and then back down at the creature that was slowly, cautiously rising back to its feet, staying well enough away from the deadly tip of the elf's dagger.

She tossed the totem to me, "What are you called?" She asked the creature in a slightly calmer voice.

Trembling, the creature answered, "I am called Bolla."

"What is your race? What are your people called?" She inquired in an even tone.

"We are called the Lacerta," Bolla answered with a natural hiss in his voice that made him slightly difficult to understand.

"Why did your friend attack me?" I asked, highly agitated.

Bolla hesitated, and then answered, "I do not know."

Balt roared and jumped closer, brandishing his teeth as well as his Great Axe, "I donna' believe ya!" He snorted, slightly startling even me.

Bolla shrank back and hissed, "I don't know! I swear!"

The lacerta took a step back to regain his footing and continued, "This is a place of worship, not war!"

Brother Fost gave out a sharp whistle and pointed to the runes carved in the wall, "What do these markings mean, Bolla?" The priest asked.

Bolla blinked once then instantly answered, "Roughly translated into your language, they mean: FATE. Or, 'The totality of one's acts in each state of one's existence.'"

Satisfied, Brother Fost added, "I too, am a holy man."

Brother Fost retrieved the totem from me and handed it to Bolla, "I hope you fully realize that we will not hesitate to cut you down where you stand, if you decide to cross us."

"I understand." The lizard-man hissed, surprised at our sudden apparent acceptance.

I picked up a sword from the floor and handed it to Bolla, "We trust you to guide us safely through these passages and caverns. No tricks!"

"Understood," Bolla answered, slightly apprehensive.

"I gots me eyes on ye!" Balt growled.

⸭

Bolla led us out through the tunnel and back to the ledge, I followed closely behind.

Sir Quinn stayed close behind me.

The rest of the group followed behind the knight, circulating positions except for Balt, who always kept up the rear with his Great Axe.

We continued down the narrow ledge-path for what seemed like a few hours, observing stalactites, which are huge icicle shaped mineral deposits hanging from the ceiling of the cavern, that in a way look quite like giant fangs.

Below, we could see the stalagmites, which are the opposite.

They are cone shaped mineral deposits built up from the floor, created by dripping water that is full of minerals.

There were also pillars, which were formed when stalactites and stalagmites meet and join together.

The sight was stunning.

The continuous sound of rushing water grew louder and louder the further we descended.

The trickling stream we once saw below from so high above had been transformed into a great rushing river, complete with white water rapids. (Up to class 5.)

The ledge-path widened out and eventually leveled to a flat grade.

Another dark tunnel loomed to our left, the only way to continue.

"Look what I found!!" Brother Fost unexpectedly piped, breaking the (almost) silence, we all quickly turned in alarm to face him.

The halfling priest stood alone, unharmed, with a gleam in his eyes as he showed off the coin he had tossed from the ledge hours ago. (We never heard it hit bottom.)

"Fortune smiles, my little friend," Bolla quipped with a hiss.

"What be through there?" Balt asked as he pointed at the dark tunnel.

"More caverns and tunnels," The lacerta holy man answered, "eventually they lead all the way to the river you see down below. It will take only a few more—"

A large dark shadow loomed overhead and then quickly moved away.

Bolla took a panicked look around and quickly drew his sword.

"What is it?" I asked, as I drew my sword as well.

The rest of the party followed suit.

"We must be cautious," Bolla hissed.

"Why's tat?" Balt invited with a wild smile upon his lips and excitement dripping from his words.

"We are about to encounter the olyame," Bolla responded.

"Who or what are the olyame?" Sir Quinn inquired reluctantly.

"The olyame are large humanoid creatures with strong leathery wings, like those of a bat.

To be more accurate, the wings resemble those of a demon or dragon.

The olyame don't really have teeth, but rather tusks that protrude from their upper jaw under their noses that act as..." Bolla paused to think of a suitable word, "... well, I guess they would act as fangs, but unlike vampires, the olyame do not drink their victim's blood. Instead, they let the blood drain away, then consume the flesh."

Meeka went ashen white and swallowed back a heave.

I thought about the information we had just received, "Bolla," I began, "do you think they have feet that are more like yours, or more like ours?" I asked as I pointed down at Brother Fost's feet, as they were the only feet like mine that were exposed.

Bolla shook his head as if to say 'neither', "Talons," he replied, "like those found on a bird of prey, such as a hawk or an eagle."

I nodded in understanding, "That would explain the strange marks on the walls and ceiling when we first entered this cave."

"As well as the lack of... What was that word you used?" Brother Fost inquired.

"Guano," I answered quickly, gaining a reaction once again from Meeka as she frowned and cringed in disgust.

I let loose a silent chuckle and playfully nudged the wizard with my elbow.

She shot me a pained look then smiled.

"Do us a favor," I said to Loher, becoming serious as I stretched my bowstring into place.

I didn't have to finish my request as the elf notched an arrow loosely onto her bowstring.

There was a series of loud clicks and snaps behind me, turning, I observed Brother Fost assembling a light crossbow.

When he completed its assembly, he loaded it with two dozen small bolts (an auto-re-loader of his own design.)

"I'm ready!" The halfling priest proudly announced.

I smiled and readied my own bow.

Meeka was quietly chanting a new spell from her tome, so I signaled the team to take a short rest to allow the wizard enough time to study and become ready.

This gave the others a chance to dredge up a sort of courage, if needed.

When the wizard was ready, we passed food and drink around and exchanged personal stories, getting to know our new companion.

Bolla began to tell us of his past; "My people are not originally from these caverns. Years ago, we thrived on the islands outside of these walls, in the sun. We were discovered by a species of creature called the Riza.

"The riza are creatures that are akin to the mer'folk, like mermaids and mermen, except the difference between the distant cousins are, while the mer'folk are half-fish half-man and tend to be on the goodish side, the riza are half-squid half-man and tend to be selfish and evil. Another difference between the two is while the mer'folk can breathe freely both in and out of the water; the riza can only breathe while submerged. The riza enslaved some mer'folk as well for communication purposes between us and them. They enslaved my tribe, among others, within these walls, to collect for them the rumored ancient dragon's treasure."

"A dragon?!" Balt excitedly interrupted.

"So sorry to disappoint," Bolla explained, "but not within these walls. The treasure the riza had found actually belongs to a faction of pirates that still roam these waters." Bolla paused to gauge our reactions; when he received none, he continued, "Once the pirates discovered that their treasure was being, as they say, 'plundered,' they began to attack my people until they learned that we were merely slaves of the riza. They then utterly slaughtered the riza almost into extinction. The lacerta and mer'folk were then released from servitude, but groups of each race decided to stay and work for the faction as 'treasure tenders,' guarding the pirates' 'Booty' as they call it. Up until now, no one has come even remotely this close to re-discovering the treasure or us."

Balt began to chuckle as if something had occurred to him, "This be ta verra reason yor friends attacked us in ta first place."

"Now that you mention it," Bolla said as an outward thought, "that makes good sense, but I swear to you, I had nothing to do with the attack! That is why I ran! I am a holy man!" He exclaimed.

"Take ease, Lizard," the dwarf laughed, "Yor in ne harm's path."

Bolla produced the bone totem and nervously rubbed it in order to calm himself.

"Shall we continue our course?" Sir Quinn inquired, breaking the still.

The team arose and gathered their weapons and gear.

The wizard closed her tome and placed it within the folds of her robes, "I feel ready for just about anything," she announced bravely, "let one of those flying freaks try to make a meal out of one of us!"

Loher giggled and gave the wizard an extremely rare smile.

"The pirates' treasure is in no danger from us," the knight reassured.

"That is good, my friend," Bolla laughed with a hiss, "that is very good... for you." He grimly warned, now serious, "There are many Lacerta warriors guarding that treasure, as well as the pirates themselves at times, and none will hesitate to kill anyone that gets too close. You will be safe with me as your escort, as long as you keep your distance from it."

We continued our walk to the dark tunnel, Bolla nervously and cautiously took a good look around, "The only things we truly have left to fear in these caverns are the olyame."

———◆———

"Illuminare!!" The wizard shouted, as she cast a spell of bright light through the tunnel.

Bolla jumped at the sudden bright flash.

A sharp fluttering, scraping sound retreated back deep into the darkness further into the tunnel – afraid of the new bright light.

"What in the Gods' names was that??" Meeka gasped.

"Hmm... The olyame," Balt guessed in a monotone voice.

"That would be correct, my stout friend," Bolla whispered.

"Stout," Balt grunted an echo.

The tunnel was wide enough for three average-sized humans to walk side-by-side as they traveled through, but we stayed safely in our single file formation with Bolla up front leading the way, myself closely after.

Sir Quinn was directly behind me, but after him it was the usual random grouping of the rest, save Balt, who always took up the rear.

Although we were quite safe in the glow of Meeka's 'light' spell, our eyes and ears were working overtime constantly searching for the elusive and very dangerous creatures known as the dreaded olyame.

Fear was not an issue, as preservation and caution took charge.

We all knew that there is safety in numbers, and we had already proven that as a group, we were a good team in a fight.

Our nerves had stayed calmer than expected in the fact that over half of us had distance weapons, which were far more effective against foes-in-flight.

The tunnel snaked this way, turned that way and twisted around in yet another, winding around as if in circles, steadily sloping in a downward spiral.

We were closing the distance, chasing the horrible scraping and fluttering sound of the nocturnal olyame, as Meeka's 'light' spell led the way.

"When my 'light' spell begins to fade, it will take me a moment to recast it again, so be ready to defend us," the wizard warned, "I'll try to give us enough fair warning before it goes out."

She then turned to face the dwarven warrior, "Balt," she said, "You may want to light a torch right now to be on the safe side."

"How much more time do we have left?" I asked, as Balt fetched a torch from his pack and lit it.

Warm firelight brightened the existing light of the wizard's spell, casting oblong shadows that danced around us, as the flames bounced and flickered.

"Ten or twelve minutes," she answered, "but that's only a guess."

We all moved steadily along.

The scraping and fluttering sounds were slowly joined once again by the roar of rushing water growing louder as we moved further towards the bottom of the tunnel.

The torchlight rapidly began to glow brighter, as Meeka's spell began to fade.

"Get ready!" The wizard warned.

Brother Fost raised his crossbow as Loher and I lightly pulled on our bowstrings.

Our elven infrared vision naturally began to overtake our sense of sight, as the darkness ensued.

"Group together!" I ordered as the spell faded to flickering torch-light.

In the narrow tunnel, we as a team did our best to stand back-to-back in a tight cluster.

Unaffected by the dim firelight, the winged olyame circled and flew in for their attack.

The only sound we heard, other than the low throb of the distant river, was the chanting from our wizard as she prepared a new 'light' spell; The olyame were unbelievably silent while in actual attack mode.

"I thought all she had to say was 'Illuma-something' and the spell would work!" Sir Quinn shouted in confusion and frustration, as he ducked under the claws of an attacking olyame.

"That is just to **cast** the spell," Brother Fost called back, as he fired off a round from his Blessed Crossbow.

An olyame screeched out in pain as the priest's Holy Bolt found its mark, "She's got to chant the incantation first!"

I pulled back on my bowstring and fired off an arrow at the closest foe.

My arrow flew true and bit in, forcing the creature to slam into the wall and skid across the floor behind us.

Its wings flapped violently as Balt's Great Axe made quick work of it, cleaving the vile creature in two.

When its wings ceased their motion, the dwarf beat his fist into his own chest and roared out in victory.

Another olyame cruised silently overhead, diving down in an attacking posture; most of its attacks were unsuccessful.

"Illuminare!" Meeka finally cried, engulfing the entire area in a blinding bright light.

Then...sudden acrid smoke.

Glorious smoke.

From the olyame's point of view: A great blinding flash of light unexpectedly erupted, staying steadily lit, blinding the creature, confusing it and burning its flesh and wings.

Painfully, it groped its way towards the safety of darkness after it slammed headlong into a wall.

Before it could successfully escape, it was stabbed and fatally pierced by the blade wielded by the Royal Knight. (The End.)

The team stood silent as we strained to listen for the sound of more creatures approaching, but all we could hear was the low ebb of the rushing water and the thunderous beating of our own hearts in our chests.

Satisfied the battle was won, a low cheer sprang forth from the lips of us seven victors.

The twin corpses that lay at our feet could not be identified as they smoldered from exposure to the wizard's powerful spell.

"Well, that explains why I have never seen one of these creatures before," I commented, "The sun would destroy them quite like it would a vampire."

I stood there, half-heartedly studying one of the bodies as the smoke rose away like stinking vapors.

I then wondered why they would not go out hunting at night, but decided to keep my thoughts silent; perhaps they did.

Once again, acrid smoke began to fill the tunnel and burn our throats and eyes.

We escaped to cleaner, fresher air.

"Is anybody hurt?" Brother Fost asked.

No one gave an affirmation.

"There really is no point in searching the bodies," Bolla announced as Loher began to do just that, "They carry no purses, no pouches, no coins or weapons."

As I looked, I could not see the entrance from where we came in, or the first dark tunnel from which Bolla had led us down the ledge-path.

We had gone down much too far.

The river rushed into this large, dimly lit cavern through an ancient cut in the wall, where the water slowly eroded the rock away, consuming layer after layer over hundreds, perhaps thousands of years; the same was true of the route the river used to escape.

"Come this way," Bolla beckoned as he led us down river.

"What lies the other way?" I asked and hooked my thumb over my shoulder gesturing behind me.

"More of the same," Bolla answered, "Tunnels, caverns, more of my people, exits to the outside world on other islands," He explained, "If one were so inclined, one could visit any number of the islands just by following the series of underwater tunnels and caverns, but I caution; Many, many dangers await unsuspecting adventurers if one chooses to venture that way."

I noticed a peak in Balt's attention at the mere mention of the word 'danger.'"

"And what, pray tell, awaits us in this direction?" Sir Quinn inquired; pointing up ahead in the direction our guide was leading us.

"Much o' ta same's me guess," Balt quipped.

"Quite the contrary, my good dwarf," Bolla countered, "The worst we'll meet going this way would be a pirate or two, but we'll not be seen by the likes of them if we're careful."

"In that case, my new friend, it seems that our tour is at its end," Sir Quinn announced, surprising us all. "We shall return to our King and report to him what we have learned."

"You are more than welcome to join us, Bolla." I offered.

The lacerta did not answer, but instead, he began to lead us back up to the ledge-path.

The journey back to the mouth of the cave was a silent one, other than the sound of the rushing, raging river so far, far, impossibly far down below.

The sound began to fade away the further and further we climbed.

⸺⟨◇⟩⟶

It took me a while to regain my sense of direction as we climbed out from the mouth of the cave.

I was not even sure at first if the sun was rising or setting yet again.

I had lost all track of time.

After a brief moment, I could plainly see that the sun was on the rise, waking up a brand new day.

I just happened to look back into the cave to see our new friend disappear around a curve in the path that led inside.

We had told him that we would most likely be returning in a while and that he should beware of explorers that might illegally enter this new cave, despite the plaque Sir Quinn had affixed near its mouth.

The plaque was an official warning claiming Royal ownership of the cave, forbidding trespass; any who disobey the warning shall be subject to punishment of death (or worse!)

Before Bolla disappeared back into the cave, he explained to us that he could not join us on our journey back to Salvus Hus, as he had his own duties to attend to.

We all said our farewells and slowly descended the face of the mountain and back to the shore.

When we finally arrived back at the shore, it was early and there was yet no sign of The Scorpion, or any other ship.

We set up camp and awaited the return of the ship... and the sun.

Food and drink were passed around, as we reflected upon the previous night's adventures.

By the time the sun was just above the lowest peaks of the surrounding mountains, The Scorpion had sailed within view.

It was towing a smaller boat along with it.

By noon, the new dock on the island was completed and the smaller ship and the construction crew had sailed away; we then were aboard The Scorpion, and on our way back to the harbor near Dewarg.

"Did 'ja find what'cha be lookin' for?" The captain asked, with an odd, uncomfortable look splayed across his face, as if he knew of some sort of a curse, legend or secret.

Sir Quinn gave him a 'None-of-your-business' look and calmly replied, "That remains to be answered, even for us," then turned away and looked off across the sea.

"I get what'cha meanin' Mon." The captain said, smiling and bobbing his head to the unheard rhythm in his own mind.

I took a leisurely stroll around the tidy ship, enjoying the breeze in my hair and the warm sun on my skin.

The motion of the ship on the wavy sea was relaxing and I could feel the stress melting—

-Suddenly, the images of that odd fairie and rabbit race quickly took over my thoughts and flooded my mind.

(Rabbits!)

I became violently dizzy and needed to sit down.

(Fairies!)

Reeling from the extreme vertigo, I stumbled about, feeling with my hands for a place to sit down and rest.

(…The group cheered on as the mounted rabbits raced…)

Almost instantly, I felt hands on my shoulders, and…

(The cheering continued…)

…I heard a familiar female voice ask me if I was alright.

(A brown and white speckled bunny claimed victory and gold was exchanged.)

I shook my head…

(Cheering…)

…unable to speak, but the hands guided me to a bench and sat me down.

The voice was soothing and convinced me to relax.

(The sounds of the start of a new race trailed off…)

A water skin was placed in my hands and gently guided to my lips.

"Drink," I heard the voice, now recognized as Meeka's, tell me.

As I drank, the noises and visions that plagued my mind melted off into The Haze.

By the time we arrived at the harbor near Dewarg, I was back up on my feet again and feeling quite well.

Meeka was looking at me with obvious worry written in her eyes.

"Perhaps she would think it was just common sea sickness." I silently hoped to myself.

"What happened back there?" Meeka asked, "That was not sea sickness, it seemed more like—"

"Damn, perhaps not." I groaned within my head.

"Hold this ship!" Sir Quinn ordered, "We will return shortly."

The captain laughed and agreed, "No worries, Mon. We wait for ja."

Reluctantly, I told Meeka about the fairies and the rabbit race and I told her about the sightings of more, or perhaps the same, fairies.

I even described the re-occurring visions of that damn race, like the one I just suffered from there on the ship.

She told me that she too, had seen the fairies by the tree at Avilyn Harbor on the day of the storm, but she had paid them no mind, assuming they were seeking shelter from the storm; still, she found it odd that they would willingly show themselves like that.

Apologizing for her eavesdropping, Loher told us that she had just remembered seeing some fairies on the night that we camped in the grove of trees after the fight in Steorra.

She said she now remembered seeing them dancing by our campfire, but quickly dismissed them as harmless, and not odd, as elves and fairies co-exist within the Seolfer Wudu; so when I asked if she had seen anything strange, it had not occurred to her that they were what I was asking about.

We decided, for now, to keep all this between just the three of us.

We arrived at the harbor's common corral, retrieved our mounts and returned to The Scorpion so we could set sail back to Avilyn Harbor.

Perhaps, but doubtful, those fairies would still be by that old tree.

On our way, the water shimmered as the sun shown upon the waves, like a million flames dancing upon a wrinkled blue-green blanket.

Above, seagulls chased around like children playing a game of tag in a wide meadow of blue.

Puffs of cottony clouds drifted lazily by, each with its own unique size and shape.

(Fairies and rabbits?!?!)

Brother Fost and one of the sailors had been fishing and caught a large amount of various species; they proudly showed off their own record sized trophies to the rest of us.

We congratulated them with handshakes and slaps on the back as the two fishermen smiled.

(Dinner was served!)

A few hours later, Avilyn Harbor appeared just off the bow of the ship closing fast, so my companions and I prepared to disembark on the rest of our journey.

At the harbor, Sir Quinn handed the captain a few coins and thanked him as we went ashore.

We started slowly for the trail back to the castle and as we passed the tree, I noticed Meeka and Loher glance at it as I did; there was nothing there.

We followed the trail south for a while until Brother Fost swiftly rode off ahead and scouted out an unseen path.

Shortly, he returned and announced, "I offer that we take a rest and have a good meal for a change!"

Balt shot him a confused look, but then drew it back and went blank again.

The rest of us looked from the priest to the fighter and then back to the priest.

"I beg your pardon, Brother Fost?" Sir Quinn requested.

"My homeland is just ahead," the priest reiterated, "we could stop and rest and have a proper meal...and drinks!"

Now, with the knowledge of a drink, the dwarven fighter's interest was piqued, "Aye! We could use some good eats an' a drink'r three!" Balt cheered happily, licking his chops.

I had to admit as well, that my own stomach had been grumbling so I whole heartedly agreed.

Sir Quinn and Meeka had not argued with the idea, while Loher remained neutral, as always.

We found ourselves being blindly led by the halfling priest of Onh to the meadows of Leah, and the lands of Hydan Seir, homeland of the halfling race.

Chapter Four

Hydan Seir

The 'path' on which Brother Fost led us was edged by a mixture of fragrant flowers.

The combination was set just so, in order to sedate and confuse non-halfling visitors or intruders.

We (all but Brother Fost) became dizzy and sleepy and began to doze off on the backs of our mounts, which seemed to not be affected by the flowers.

Shortly, (I think) we emerged into a widespread meadow, green, dotted with thousands of light blue flowers.

It looked as though one of the Gods had dropped a handful of sapphires across a lush green carpet.

The meadow was ornately lined with ash, poplar and birch trees, which were filled with what seemed like millions of birds that were singing together in perfect harmony, like a choir, as small animals of every kind cavorted safely in play below.

The area was utterly tranquil... almost like my home in the Seolfer Wudu.

The wind was so calm, relaxing and temperate, that it didn't upset or disturb the butterflies that flitted from flower to flower, along with the busy bees.

Faintly, I could just make out the trickling sounds of a small stream somewhere in the distance.

Everything looked so peaceful, so wonderful, so—

I saw them!

I quickly reached over and tapped Meeka on her back, while I held my other index finger over my pursed lips in a quieting gesture.

She slowly, silently leaned near to look over my shoulder, as if to see in my exact point of view.

I pointed my finger and she followed my gaze; Loher was now looking too.

Off by a patch of mushrooms and toadstools, looking out and over at us, was a group of a half-dozen (or more) fairies.

Meeka waved...

One waved back.

I waved...

Nothing.

They were gone as if they were never even there.

The three of us were left standing there blinking at each other not saying a word...

Had we really seen them?

Were they really there?

What does this mean?

We turned to catch up with the rest of the group so we wouldn't get lost amongst the hidden paths and trails.

I took one last look behind us to see if the fairies had returned, but noticed they had not.

Hydan Seir was finally revealed to us as we passed through an opening in the copse of thick trees that apparently surrounded the shire.

The land within was unnaturally hilly and even more so unnaturally green.

Dark dirt paths twisted this way and that way among the hills and oddly spaced out ancient looking (and very large) oak and maple trees.

Upon further examination, I could see that there were ornately carved heavy wooden doors – some adorned with glass windows – affixed into the side of each hill, as if it was hollowed out to create a (cave) semi-subterranean dwelling.

Wooden fences carefully marked off apparent property lines (how quaint).

In the center of the shire, an obnoxiously large stone structure had been erected.

This beautifully crafted structure housed five different compartments...

1. A school: The halfling race is well convinced, and rightly so, that an education is the key to a productive, happy, healthy and harmonious long life; halflings are by far the most intelligent race within the Realm of Beornan Heafod.

2. A market: Where the citizens of Hydan Seir would go to purchase their food, clothing, furniture, etc. all of which were grown, raised and fabricated locally within the shire's borders; the halfling race is very self-sufficient.

3. A civic center: Citizens of the shire could go enjoy a concert performance or play; Council Meetings are held here as well.

4. The Abbey of Onh: A church where citizens could congregate and worship; also the place where the priests of Onh

lived and learned the ways of Onh.

This was Brother Fost's home.

Last (and least,)

5. An inn/livery stable: Very rarely used and crammed into the very back of the structure, the guests of the shire could stay here, if not invited to stay with their hosts.

One could not just simply 'stumble' into the shire.

A tavern called 'The Shoe' – Ironically named because halflings do not wear shoes, stood apart from the inn/stable.

It stood apart because the halflings thought it disrespectful to have such a place physically connected to a church and school. (This says a lot for the stable!)

A large cemetery took up a far, dark corner of the shire; the headstones were also ornate and large.

We stowed our mounts in the livery stable making sure they were watered, fed and rubbed down properly.

After checking ourselves into the inn, (all but Brother Fost, who went home to the abbey,) we joined up again at 'The Shoe' for an evening meal.

'The Shoe' was unusually empty which was odd, especially for the halfling race who loves their food and drink.

The only patrons in the tavern were an elderly grey-haired human male wearing white robes, speaking with a young halfling male wearing elven chainmail armor; a bored looking barmaid was at the other end of the bar, trying to stay busy.

The man and the halfling's conversation looked intense and extremely private; however, I did manage to overhear something about a ring of sorts.

"I thought I knew everyone in the shire, but I'm afraid I don't know him." Brother Fost casually remarked about the armor clad halfling at the bar, as we took our seats at a table near the fire. (It was the table in the northwest corner.)

"Fost Atlberry!" A female voice sounded from across the room.

We all turned to see the barkeep swiftly striding across the tavern with her arms wide and a smile upon her face, "Welcome home, Brother Fost!" she cried.

"How are you Marta?" Brother Fost called back and stepped toward her.

They embraced in a friendly hug.

"What can I get for you and your friends?" Marta asked, wide-eyed at the rest of us.

We all told her what we wanted, most of our orders were the same; Brother Fost and Marta sat and reminisced for a moment, then she disappeared behind the bar.

The tavern was quite cozy, although the chairs proved to be a bit small and the ceiling was also a bit too low, so anyone that stood taller than five feet tall had to walk hunched over while indoors.

The fire was warm and inviting, the food was filling, and the stout and ale went down smoothly, but the best of all was the conversation.

The two at the bar had left, leaving the tavern to ourselves, so then finally alone, we could freely speak of our journey thus far.

After some time, I noticed that Loher had given Meeka an anomalous look, then they both turned their gaze upon me; I knew exactly what they were thinking.

Sir Quinn noticed their looks as well, "What's this all about?" The knight asked quite curiously.

After a bit of hesitation, I slowly began to explain my odd fairie/rabbit flashbacks and the multiple sightings the three of us had each witnessed.

Brother Fost admitted to observing the fairies at Avilyn Harbor.

Balt told us he remembered seeing the fairies and rabbits together while we were leaving the Royal town of Salvus Hus on our first day of our journey; a sighting I was not a witness to.

Sir Quinn had seen the fairies that I had pointed to as we entered the shire just a few hours ago.

"If you hadn't pointed at them, I probably wouldn't have ever seen them." The knight added, "I'm not very observant of such things." He laughed.

"What, if anything, do you think all this means?" I generally asked my companions around the table.

We all sat there, pondering the question over another few rounds of drinks and well on into the night but came up with no solid answers.

We decided to call it a night as both Meeka and Brother Fost had each yawned into the backs of their hands and wiped tired tears from their eyes.

We each pooled in some coins to pay the tab, and then made our way to the door and out into the still of the night.

While Brother Fost adjourned to his place at the abbey, Meeka and Loher chose to share a room at the inn.

Balt, Sir Quinn and I each retired to our own respective rooms as well.

———◦———

I closed the door to my room, removed my gear, and then sat on the edge of my bed.

Visions from the new cave and of Bolla, the lacerta holy man, swam through my mind.

Brother Fost's coin seemed to have never hit bottom.

(We counted…)

The white water river looked like a trickling stream at first so far, far down below.

So many thoughts…

So many memories…

So many concerns…

So many—

("Why did your friend attack me?!")

We should have gone in further and actually seen the pirates and their treasure.

("I do not know!")

We should have explored the cave a lot more.

("This is a place of worship, not war!!")

We should have—

There was a knock at my door…

—spoken to the mer'folk.

'Where is my crystal dagger?'

I palmed an old iron dagger from my gear on the floor and then slowly cracked open the door.

Peeking outside, I saw Sir Quinn and Balt, so I opened the door wider and invited the pair in.

"Ye weren't asleepin' yet, were ye?" The dwarf asked as he plopped down on the foot of my bed.

"No, not yet," I answered, "I was just sitting here thinking that we should have explored the cave a bit more thoroughly."

I casually hid the old iron dagger back amid my gear.

"That is precisely what we are here to discuss with you, Thunor." The knight explained, "I decided to pull us out of the cave because I felt that we were unprepared to face a ship full of pirates."

"Aye," the dwarven fighter agreed, and then added, "An' who's ta say that there really are pirates, an' na truly a livin' dragon? Tat lizard may've been try'n ta trick us."

As I stood there, I took in all of the given information and pondered the possibilities.

After a thoughtful moment, I agreed with the knight's decision to evacuate.

We sat and idly chatted for a while, taking sips of whatever the dwarf had in his flask, (it was stiff, strong and smelled a lot like cat urine,) then the two got up and drunkenly stumbled to the door. (More Sir Quinn than Balt.)

Balt bid me a good night and walked out of the room, while Sir Quinn turned back and soberly added, "If I put together an attachment of men to go back and fully explore and map out that cave, I hope you would be willing to join me as my lead ranger."

"I would be honored, Sir Knight." I agreed.

"The final decision would, of course, belong to the King," the knight admitted, "but I would like to have all of my ducks in a row, so to speak, when the question arises."

"Count me in." I confirmed.

The knight clapped me on the back and then returned back to his room for a good night's rest.

I paced my room for another hour or so and then finally lay down.

As I laid there trying to fall asleep, thoughts of pirates, dragons and treasure still floated around in my head.

I must have finally dozed off because I awoke drenched in sweat, my heart racing, dream quickly fading...

The dream was of being in a dry desert region, (I have no idea who was with me, as everyone was blurred, as dreams often do,) we were standing by a ridge or some sort of low mesa with an odd overhang that we were standing under, perhaps to keep out of the sun.

There was a cavern like hole in the ceiling of this overhang that was large enough to easily crawl into if you could hoist your body up into it.

One of my blurry companions actually tried crawling up into the hole, but was chased out by a man-sized black antlike creature that bit the blurry man's arm.

The blurry bite victim screamed in pain, grabbed his arm and ran off into the bright sun.

I took one of my two whips from my belt, (I do not own any whips,) and vanquished the creature with one expert (yeah, right) crack from the whip.

Then I ran out into the blinding sunlight to find my injured blurry friend; I eventually found him while he was in the process of transforming into some sort of half-man, half-monkey type creature.

When the metamorphosis was finally complete, which was horrifying and seemed to have taken forever, the monkey-creature seemed to be...

...Happy to be that way.

Suddenly a dark shape loomed overhead and blotted out the light of the sun; I woke up from the dream drenched in sweat and extremely shaken.

I don't really know what happened after the appearance of the looming dark shape, but apparently it was traumatic enough for me to repress the memories of it.

I sat bolt upright in my bed for a while confused and shaking, trying desperately to remember exactly where I was; the room was still dark and had a strange pungent odor to it.

I got out of bed and went over to the window to look outside. (From the time I awoke until the time I found myself looking out the window, was no less than ten minutes.)

The sun was just barely beginning to show behind the dense tree line.

As I looked out at what I could see from my window, which was not much as I saw a brick and fieldstone wall blocking most of the view, off to the left I could just barely make out a sliver of a cemetery.

I finally began to remember that we were in the halfling shire, Hydan Seir, Brother Fost's home.

I sat back down on the bed again, and again tried to gather my thoughts.

That strange monkey-man dream from just moments ago was still squishing around in my grey matter.

I must have dozed off again, because I was awoken again by yet another sharp rapping at my door.

I quickly got up and looked through the window to see Loher standing there waiting patiently, the usual blank stare upon her pretty face.

I opened the door wide to let her in, but despite the smile she almost showed and quickly hid away, she politely refused and stood outside.

She proceeded to inform me that the rest of the team was meeting at 'The Shoe' for breakfast in fifteen minutes.

I nodded, and then she swiftly walked away.

Ten minutes later, I walked into 'The Shoe' and almost bumped into a very old, very plump, very happy and very well dressed halfling.

We politely excused each other and I entered the tavern.

After a brief moment of sight adjustment due to the extreme change from bright sunlight to dim firelight, I located my friends sitting at the same table we were sitting at just a few hours before; it occurred to me that it had been the same table and the same exact seats we all took, no matter which tavern we were visiting.

I looked around after I took my seat and took a long pull from the drink Loher had handed me, "I took the liberty of ordering this for you," she said with a beautiful and rare smile that quickly was hidden away.

I noticed that there was a large crew of halflings erecting a crude stage away from the door and near the bar.

"What's going on here?" I asked as I hooked a thumb over my shoulder, pointing at the stage.

"The mayor is setting up for a show tonight." Brother Fost replied.

"A show at 'The Shoe,'" Meeka giggled.

"That's the Mayor," Brother Fost announced as the same well dressed, happy, old and very plump halfling I almost ran over, walked back into the tavern, "Doogan Diggats, the Mayor of Hydan Seir, is one of the original founding fathers of this hidden shire.

He was once a very famous Royal Bard for King Lagu Ofer'Eal's father and grandfather alike.

As a bard, Diggats was mussically proficient with the lyre, which is a harp-like instrument, the guitarish lute, zither and their larger cousin, the sitar, as well as the pan flute.

He was unanimously elected as Mayor of Hydan Seir not only because of his Royal ties, which quite honestly were enough alone, or because of his standing as one of the founding fathers, but also because he single handedly vanquished one of Beornan Heafod's rarest, but not unheard of, creatures known as a Xobish.

A Xobish is an extremely large and extremely dangerous bumble bee like creature, which is roughly the size and weight of your basic adult tom cat.

The battlefield was right here on the very spot that the shire sits now; yes, this entire area.

As legend states, the one-on-one battle took an estimated eighteen hours, or more accurately, from just after sun up, until just before twilight.

The Mayor is the only one that truly knows how long the battle took, but it made him a local folk hero and has quickly become a legend." Brother Fost finally finished and took a long deserved pull from his own drink.

Balt, with a toothy grin upon his face and blinking wildly mused, "Methinks that be th' most I ever hear'ed ye say at one time, Priest."

The halfling laughed and munched a biscuit.

"Are we going to stay and see the show... in 'The Shoe'?" I asked, and winked at Meeka, who quickly commenced giggling.

The halfling priest quickly shot a questioning glance at the knight who simply shrugged, "Would you all like to stay to watch the show?" He asked.

"In 'The Shoe'," Meeka giggled once again.

The whole party happily agreed.

"So be it!" The priest announced, "What do we do until then?"

"You could show us around the shire," Loher suggested.

"Or..." Balt started with a mysterious look in his eyes, "we could take this day an' go a-lookin' fer yer wee beasties that be stirrin' up s'much trouble by hangin' about."

The party looked around from face to face and pondered this suggestion for a moment...

"Personally, I think Balt has a great idea." Sir Quinn reflected.

"As do I," I agreed.

"I could show you around as we look for our 'friends', so it makes no difference to me." Brother Fost said.

Meeka and Loher just shrugged.

"Let's go an' find 'em!" Balt growled with enthusiasm.

<hr>

"Well, this is where we saw them." I rhetorically announced, splaying my hand at the small patch of mushrooms and toadstools just outside the entrance to the shire proper.

Meeka and Loher silently nodded their heads in agreement, while Brother Fost had a thoughtful look upon his face.

The knight and the fighter just stood aside and observed.

"Do ye see any sign o' them, Ranger?" Balt asked.

I carefully looked around and found fading evidence that the 'wee folk' had been there, but they apparently moved on shortly after our sighting.

I followed the tracks as best as I could, but it had become quite difficult due to the fact that they had taken flight several times and I had to find their landing spots; shortly, I had lost all traces of their movements.

"I'm afraid our plan has failed." I reluctantly announced.

"I have an idea!" Meeka offered excitedly and quickly started chanting a memorized spell.

We all unconsciously took a step away.

After a moment, the wizard raised her hands level with the ground and commanded, "Ostendere me quod latet!"

Immediately, a semi-invisible path stretched from the mushroom patch, through the air, to a flower patch, then to a tree branch.

The path then went from that tree branch to a mound of dirt, from there, it bounced from flower to flower as if it was chasing a pollinating bumble bee.

(Xobish!)

The game of tag must have ended because the path ended up crossing over to another clump of mushrooms and then up to the lower branch of a tree, where standing on this branch, completely unaware that he was visible, stood a male sprite, munching on a raspberry, juice oozing down his arm.

The sprite stood there, watching us, quite confident he had not been seen until it was too late...

...Meeka turned toward him and took an obvious step in his direction, looking directly at him.

The sprite panicked and took flight to the branch of a different tree, but Loher anticipated this move and cunningly captured him in her leather-bound gloved hand.

Just as the elven maiden predicted, the sprite attempted to bite and claw his way to freedom, but failed.

"Take ease, my friend, take ease." Loher cooed to the sprite, "I'll not harm you, take ease."

The sprite continued to claw and bite for his freedom, but after a moment, he grew tired and gave up.

"What is this madness!?" The sprite commanded.

"Take ease," Loher repeated softly, "I will set you free if you calm and not flee if I do so."

The sprite struggled again, "I do not believe you!" he growled with a mouth full of glove.

"Then I'll just hold you like this until you tire enough to be calm." Loher laughed, but the sprite found no humor in her words and fought harder.

"Th' wee laddy's bound ta hurt 'imself if 'e's na careful." Balt commented, slightly impressed with the sprite's fighting will.

We waited once more for the sprite to settle down enough to calmly communicate with and when he finally did, we began our informal investigation...

"We truly have no wish to harm you good Sprite, we only wish—" Sir Quinn began, but was interrupted.

"I do not believe you," The sprite weakly repeated, too tired to continue the fight.

"Look 'it here, Wee One," Balt said, "if we wanted ta hurt ya; we'd 'av did it by now, doon'cha think?"

The captive sprite looked as if he was going to start up the struggle once again, but then got a thoughtful look upon his tiny face, looked up at Loher and said, "Then why, pray tell, have you tricked and trapped me?"

"We would like to know why a troupe of fairies has been sneaking around and following us... and not even being careful about staying hidden." I stated.

The sprite angrily spat out, "I, you ignorant fool, am not a fairie, I'm a sprite. And just because I'm small like my even smaller cousins, you assume that I would just automatically know the answer??"

"Not necessarily," I countered with a smile, "You could very easily gain that knowledge for us..."

"What makes you think I would do that for you?" The sprite asked, still angry.

"Because we never thought you wouldn't." I smiled.

The sprite looked at me oddly, at first, as if I had grown an extra head, but then that look slowly cleared away and was replaced with a thoughtful grin, "I'll do it," the sprite finally agreed, his smile widening, "But you will owe me a favor..."

"What will we call you, Sprite?" I asked, smiling.

"I am called Brendt."

"You have yourself a deal, Brendt." I answered and nodded my head at Loher.

She opened her hand to set the sprite free, but Brendt just stood there for a moment to straighten his clothes and dust himself off.

"You'll owe me." He laughed before he tapped his fingers of his right hand quickly to his forehead just above his right eye in a sort of a salute; he then took off in flight quicker than my eyes would allow my vision to follow...he was gone.

⸺◆⸺

The Mayor of Hydan Seir, Doogan Diggats, along with three other very young halflings that were obviously his students, were performing their recital of music, poetry and song, upon the makeshift stage in 'The Shoe'; they were just beginning their final set for the evening.

The Mayor, proficient in many instruments, was playing the sitar; a young woman was doing a hauntingly good job playing the pan flute, while the two young men were satisfactorily playing, one on a lyre and the other, a percussion instrument quite like bongos.

'The Shoe' was packed, standing room only, and other than Fost and Balt, we all had an easy time observing the show over the heads of the much shorter crowd.

The final song for the evening was a local favorite and was joined in by almost every voice in the tavern.

Originally, the song was sung just a single time through, but it was so loved by all, that it continued three more times in a row with no pause.

This song was titled: 'Xobish' and was about Mayor Diggats' encounter with the named legendary beast…

"The morning was bright and shiny—

The air was crisp and clean—

I thought I'd do some fishing—

I strolled along the stream—

I heard a buzz and the Xobish tried to sting me on my leg—

I was forced to face the Xobish.

Down from the sky, the Xobish flew—

From my belt, my dagger I drew—

I was forced to fight the Xobish.

The sky was black and starry—

The meadow, dark and red—

My body, it was tired—

The Xobish, it was dead—

Its corpse I drug back to the town, a hero I became—

I was forced to kill the Xobish." (end.)

At the end of the fourth time through the song, the crowd erupted into applause.

Mayor Diggats and his students took a bow, and then he introduced each student once again.

An announcement was made that the drinks were on the house for the rest of the night.

Most of the elderly and all of the very young patrons left the tavern, leaving our usual table available; we sat and ordered a round of drinks.

"It's not very often we have visitors of another race here within the natural walls of our beloved shire," an elderly voice announced from across the emptying tavern.

Brother Fost quickly stood erect, his eyes wide and a smile snapped upon his lips.

"May I sit with you and your interesting companions, Brother Fost?" The Mayor asked as he crossed the room and reached our table.

"Mayor Diggats, Your Honor!" Brother Fost smiled, "It would bring my friends and me great happiness if you would indeed join us!"

We all respectfully rose to our feet and allowed the Mayor to sit first, drink in hand.

"So, what do we have here?" The Mayor asked, regarding the team with wide, curious eyes.

Brother Fost introduced us all, one by one, and then stated, "We are on a Royal mission for the King, Lagu Ofer'Eal."

"Intriguing," the Mayor said, licking his lips in interest and excitement.

Marta, the barmaid, appeared at our table to refresh our drinks, and then hurried away to the bar with our order.

"A royal mission, you say?" The Mayor repeated thoughtfully, "A mission that brought you here to the shire?"

Before anyone could say another word, Olphyn, the owner and lead barkeep of 'The Shoe,' appeared at our table with our fresh drinks.

"Olphyn," The Mayor nudged with genuine excitement, "We have a team of Royal adventurers among us, we do!"

Olphyn's eyes grew wide and the suddenly star-struck barkeep sat down calling, "Marta, bring me a stout, would ya please? Hmmph!"

"A Royal mission," the Mayor echoed for the barkeep's benefit. "That brought you here to the shire?"

"Must be very important. Hmmph!" The barkeep murmured.

"The mission itself didn't bring us necessarily into the shire," Brother Fost explained, patting his hand on the table on the word 'shire', "I brought my friends into the shire to take some rest and relaxation...and for a proper meal or a few."

"A might fine mess o' food ye serve 'ere, Mr. Olphyn," Balt complemented and clapped the barkeep on the shoulder, "Mighty tasty!"

"Mmm hmmph..." The barkeep grunted and smiled.

"A man o' many words," Balt quipped under his breath to me with a wink.

I had to bite back a laugh, although Meeka overheard him and could not contain her giggle.

The evening ended shortly after we relayed what we all felt was safe enough to volunteer of our mission thus far.

The elder pair of halflings seemed quite pleased and impressed with our multi-faceted adventure.

We finished our drinks, thanked the two, and then retired to our rooms at the inn. (I happened to stumble in a rare drunken stupor most of the way.)

CHAPTER FIVE

THE GAMBIT

Morning.

A rooster crowed.

"Shut Up!" An old man yelled, and then there was a loud thump of an unknown projectile, like a boot, being thrown at the rooster, which deflected off of a wooden fence.

(Silence.)

Although I was awake, I was still lying comfortably in bed, fully aware that we would soon be back on the road to Salvus Hus.

Faintly, I could hear laughter...

I sat up—

—and then I went right back down again.

(Spinning.)

Spinning, even as I lay flat on my back, searing pain rolled through my head like an out of control wildfire.

I then realized why I was left alone to sleep so late; everyone else (perhaps) was hung over as well, 'paying' for all of the 'free' drinks from the night before.

Laughing...

Balt...

Of course, the dwarf was fine...

Dwarves are somehow impervious to hangovers.

The dwarf's laughter was getting louder...

I groaned...

Balt, the 'good' fellow, was going from door-to-door checking up on each of us...

I groaned again.

I heard the door to the next room over click shut even over the hideous dwarven laughter, louder and louder still, that relentless roaring, rolling laughter was now right at my door...

Another groan escaped my throat.

Laughter and pounding on my door, as well as inside of my head; I couldn't tell which was which.

I smiled my best fake smile, "Oh, won't you come in?" I tried my best to joyfully sing...

The laughter faded a bit as the door swung open.

Balt took one look at me and roared out with laughter again, "An' 'ow be yer 'ead tis foin, foin marnin' Laddy?" He roared with great hysterics.

"I was alright until you came in," I half lied. (My human half.)

"We'll be meet'n down to ta 'Shoe' whenever ye git there." The dwarf laughed, "Hair o' ta doggie tat bit ye!" He laughed again.

I noticed Loher standing by my door behind Balt; she took a step in as the dwarf exited my room.

She took another step in and closed the door.

After the laughter finally faded away, I propped myself up on one elbow and rubbed my throbbing head with my free hand.

I looked at the elven maiden curiously.

She bent down, picked up my clothes, rolled them up into a ball and lobbed it at me, "Get up, McLaaud," she said, "I'm hungry, and I'm **not** going down there without you."

I studied her even more curiously, trying to read her, "Does this mean we're...

...Friends?" I asked, half teasing (my elven half this time.)

"Shut up!" She quipped, showing a rare smile.

"Drink this." Balt suggested, no longer laughing, as he handed me a mug of a dark, thick, steaming hot liquid; its aroma alone was enough to (wake the dead) open your eyes wide, "Ye may wanna do it quick-like." He plugged his nose with his thumb and forefinger, the rest of the fingers on that hand splayed out like a fan; he then stuck out his tongue in an awful grimace and pantomimed with his other hand by his mouth, the act of drinking.

Loher, with no obvious sign of a hangover, lightly giggled.

If the elven maiden indeed had a hangover, she was holding up better than anyone else in the group, besides Balt.

I picked up the hot steaming mug and raised it to my mouth; I could feel the steam crawl from the surface of the liquid, like a hot ghostly hand that grabbed my upper lip and pulled.

I drew some of the drink into my mouth and let it slowly flow down the back of my throat; the taste was bitter, yet pleasant.

I drank more... and then more, my heart began to race and a thin film of sweat broke out upon my brow.

Eagerly, I drank more and more until finally the mug was drained.

"How do you feel now, McLaaud?" Loher asked.

My head was clear, the hangover was gone, in fact, I couldn't remember the last time I felt so alert, or even remotely as good, "I...feel...GREAT!" I answered, and excitedly asked, "What **is** this stuff?"

Balt's face suddenly twisted in confusion, "Methinks it be called..." The dwarf thought about it for a moment and then answered, "Coffee."

"Well!" I started, as I waved over the barmaid, "I would care for some more..." The barmaid walked up to the table, "Coffee." I ordered.

The barmaid nodded, took my mug and walked away to the bar.

Shortly, the rest of the team slowly stumbled in as the barmaid returned with my coffee, "Coffees all around." I told her.

The barmaid nodded again with a smile and returned to the bar...

———◆———

My body had a strange yet comforting buzzing feel to it and my heart was still racing as my team and I mounted up and headed toward the exit of the hidden shire.

I felt awake and aware of so much more than I was normally used to.

As we passed the area where we had seen the fairies and had our encounter with Brendt, the sprite, I looked to see if anyone was there.

There was no one.

We continued on with the sun now high in the sky.

The trip from the shire, back to the open trail seemed shorter than it did on the way in, even though we were asleep through most of it.

We turned south when we reached the path-well-traveled and continued on our way back to the Royal Castle Town of Salvus Hus.

As we pressed on, we spoke of the lacerta, supposed pirates, and dragon's treasure, as well as the awesome storm and the trip through the mines of Ferrum Mons.

Time seemed to flow by quickly until the coffee buzz wore off, and then it was back to life as usual.

The sun was dipping low in the western sky and the town of Powell could be seen not far up ahead.

Sir Quinn slowed his horse and raised his hand, as a gesture for us to also slow.

A moment later, we were all stopped and standing mounted in a tight circle on the outskirts of Powell, just outside the gates.

"Night is quickly falling upon us, as you all can plainly see," the knight began, "Do we elect to continue on through the night to reach our destination quickly, do we retire to Powell's Inn, or perhaps we could set up and camp in that grove of trees over there?" The knight offered and motioned to a grove of trees not far off in the distance.

"How much further until we reach Salvus Hus?" Meeka inquired; the sun was now lower in the sky and it casted long shadows.

"If we stop here, now, and we rest until first light," I began, "we could reach the castle by tomorrow evening."

"And if we continue on now?" Brother Fost asked.

"Early afternoon," the knight answered, "at the latest."

The last rays of sunlight were slowly fading away as Loher spoke up and announced, "We have the time to kill."

"Ta she-elf speaks ta truth." Balt agreed with a wink.

Our minds were quickly made up by a terrified shriek that erupted from within the walls of the town.

We all looked at each other in alarm, as a second and much closer scream splintered out of the darkness.

Wordlessly, we galloped into town while my night vision naturally focused to life, and began to etch out faint traces of movement within the growing shadows of the town.

"Look!" Loher cried out, "Over there!" She was pointing down a dark lane.

My eyes quickly followed the path of her pointing finger and I saw the shape of a human (I assumed it was female from the scream) being carried away by another humanoid creature, that let off little to no body heat.

(Troll?... Skeleton???)

As I quickly gave chase, the sounds of my companions following could be heard close behind me.

As we moved closer, we could see that the angry townsfolk had nearly trapped the kidnapper near the town gates – then – Brother Fost cried, "Vampire!"

From the distance I was at, the vampire looked just like a normal human male with a young human girl slung over his left shoulder.

It was viciously clawing at the air between it and the townsfolk, hissing curses as it looked for escape.

Swiftly, the vampire crouched down, low to the ground, and then, with a strenuous leap, girl in tow, it jumped up into the air and seemed to dive over the crowd and out through the gates of the town.

"Come on!" Brother Fost cried as he reared his horse into motion and we all gave chase again, leaving the town and its people behind – angry and shouting.

The vampire took to its heels as quickly as its feet touched the ground, but Meeka was quicker and cast a volley of fireballs into the path of the fleeing villain; it stopped, turned and faced us.

"Let the girl go!" The halfling priest commanded.

The vampire hissed.

A low ground fog was beginning to creep from the lower parts of the land, crawling out over the area like ghostly hands with skeletal fingers.

The constant cry of a distant whippoorwill drowned out the shrill chirps of thousands of crickets looking for their mates.

I quickly jumped down from my horse, while Brother Fost and Sir Quinn followed suit.

Brother Fost quickly began to bless each and every bolt that was loaded on his crossbow and I could hear Meeka chanting a spell from somewhere behind us.

The vampire opened its mouth in a menacing, grizzly smile.

Its lips pulled back over its teeth, showing incisors and canines that reminded me of a tom cat I once had as a child; they were sparkling pinkish white and looked to be dagger sharp.

The vampire's smile drew up into haunting eyes that were red rimmed, sunken in and black like the dead eyes of a doll.

"Don't look at its eyes!" The priest called out as a warning, "Do not look it in the eyes!" He repeated and continued to call out to us.

Quickly, I lowered my gaze and noticed a few hundred rats moving about the vampire's feet, creating the odd effect of a shadow; the rats pooled around it like some sort of large carpet of flesh and fur.

The wind picked up and carried the nefarious rank stench of carrion.

Clouds moved across the sky, threatening to cover up the sliver of the moon that closely resembled a cat's eye; making it difficult to see in the gathering gloom.

"Shouldn't we have a full moon for an occasion such as this?" I quipped, trying to lessen my own fear.

The vampire's smile widened and it let out a ghoulish laugh; apparently it, but no one else, thought what I had said was funny.

"Let the girl go!" Brother Fost commanded again.

The vampire quickly canceled its smile, hissed, drew the girl back and then violently threw her at the priest, landing her on him with a bone breaking crash; his crossbow was knocked out of reach.

"Be careful what you wish for, Holy Man!" The vampire gurgled in a voice that was as un-human as the howl of a wolf.

I slowly took a step forward toward the vampire.

The vampire took a step forward toward me.

I stepped to my left, toward the fallen priest.

The vampire stepped to its right. (My left.)

Meeka's chanting had stopped and I could feel a strange sort of tingling sensation on the back of my neck, down through my spine and out through my feet.

Fireflies began to blink everywhere around us, apparently unafraid of the undead creature in their midst.

I could feel the vampire's gaze trying to burn a hole deep into my soul, trying (and failing) to make me look into its eyes.

I slid to my left a bit more... (Monkey see...)

The vampire slid to its right as well... (Monkey do.)

The tingling in my body began to spread into my arms and then into my hands and fingers.

I felt a sharp shock in my left hand that made me jump a bit. (Simon says...)

The vampire did nothing. (This was all happening very quickly...)

I decided to take a chance and dive for Brother Fost's Blessed Crossbow, as I could see it from the corner of my eye.

Meeka must have foreseen my every move, because as soon as I dove for the Blessed Crossbow, the vampire quickly moved forward toward me. (Or tried to.)

As soon as the vampire made its move, (when I made **my** move,) Meeka made her move and cast a 'lightning' spell that arced across the expanse and engulfed the vampire, knocking it away from Brother Fost and myself.

I landed in a tuck-and-roll with the Blessed Crossbow firmly in my hand.

The vampire had landed on its back with rats scattering everywhere, they were fleeing, and escaping further danger.

I stood up...

The vampire stood up.

I pulled the crossbow's trigger, launching a Holy Bolt at the undead fiend, which bounced harmlessly off a hidden armor plate under the vampire's clothes, protecting its vital, yet unbeating heart.

The vampire laughed again, bearing sharp, jagged teeth that looked nastier this time than they did the last.

Loher let loose an arrow that buried itself into the vampire's right shoulder.

The vampire hissed and yanked the arrow out.

I fired off another Holy Bolt, finding purchase in the vile creature's neck.

Vaporous smoke escaped from the wound.

The vampire shrieked out in pain, but yanked that bolt out as well.

It looked as though the vampire was going to make a sudden move to attack, when unexpectedly, a large mass of the fireflies swarmed around its face. (Fireflies?)

Balt and Sir Quinn took this chance to rescue Brother Fost and the unconscious girl, and drag them off into the safety within the walls of Powell.

Meeka began to round up our mounts.

I quickly realized that the fireflies were not fireflies at all, but fairies and the sprite, Brendt!

More and more of the tiny glowing creatures arrived in full force and surrounded the vampire, engulfing its entire body, slowly at first, but then as they became a larger group, they became stronger and stronger.

The vampire howled in anger and confusion, cursing violently as it began to try to escape by changing into a vapor cloud.

"I'll make you **pay**... with your **soul**, Ranger!!" The vampire promised as it escaped, mixing into the fog and mist, vaporizing away.

"Quickly!" Loher cried as she grabbed my hand and pulled me back into the safe walls of Powell.

Meeka was not far behind us with our mounts in tow.

I collapsed on the floor; my nerves had taken a temporary vacation.

My mouth felt as if it was stuffed with cotton and my whole body was numb.

As I laid there with the side of my face pressed down against the cool, smooth wooden floor, Brendt walked up to me and faced me in a rare eye-to-eye stance; he was grinning, his mouth full of jagged crooked teeth that almost reminded me of those in the mouth of the vampire.

"Thank you, my new friend," I said to the sprite as he stood inches away from my nose, "Now I owe you two."

"Consider that one a gift," Brendt laughed, "It was the fairies that went after the blood sucker, not me," he admitted, "I'm not immune to the bite of the undead like the fairies are."

"You can be turned into a vampire?" Meeka asked, shocked, her eyes wide.

The sprite let out a nervous chuckle, "I don't know for sure, but I'm not willing to take any chances."

I got up off the floor and stretched, my body sang out with various pops and snaps, and then I sat on the edge of a bed next to Meeka.

"Well, thank you anyway, friend." Sir Quinn commented as he walked across the room.

"Your priest will recover handsomely," a tiny voice announced right next to my ear, "we healed him, but soon, he will need to rest."

I turned my head to look in the direction of the voice, but all I saw was Meeka, smiling and pointing at my own shoulder.

I narrowed my gaze and saw a beautiful female fairie perched on my shoulder near my cheek, she smiled and waved with a finger wiggling twinkle.

"The human girl?" I asked in a low smooth whisper.

"In body, she will be fine, but in spirit and mind, she may take a while to recover," the fairie answered, "Your priest and my people are helping her now.

"I need to go talk to her family," I stated.

The fairie took graceful flight and flitted around the room.

"I shall attend to that," the knight countered, "I am human, let us not take a chance of an unfortunate racial barrier, as your looks favor your elven half. I apologize, my friend."

Reluctantly, I agreed with a slight sinking feeling inside.

The good Sir Knight bowed low, stood straight, spun around with a precise click of his heels and then exited the room to see to his task.

At some point, the wee folk vanished as well.

We were given a large room to use as our "recuperation station" as Meeka liked to call it, to rest up and heal after our heroic encounter with "The dark knight of the undead," as Brother Fost so nicely dubbed the vampire.

Townsfolk were stopping by to thank us and see if there was anything we needed.

We happily accepted all that was offered.

Balt was happy, visiting the local tavern, called 'The Lounge' with a hearty group of men.

(So much for a racial barrier.)

Brother Fost had returned from healing the girl and was now peacefully asleep, recovering from his own wounds; Meeka sat near him, keeping a close watch.

Sir Quinn was away, speaking with and consoling the young girl's family and friends.

Brendt and his army of fairies had disappeared to wherever it is that they went to; it is always such a mystery with the wee folk.

This time I was quite confident that they would return...

... Eventually.

I had finally lain down comfortably on a bed to get some well-deserved (and badly needed) rest, while Loher stood sentry, just inside the door to our room.

Sleep and dream was a welcome state, as I could feel it slowly creep up and cover me in its warm, soft and comforting embrace.

The comfort and warmth did not last long as it was replaced with the screams of the human girl, as she was carried out of the apparently not-so-safe town that she called her home.

I had to re-witness the horrifying ordeal of her being tossed through the air like a weightless rag doll, just to land hard on our halfling priest.

The vampire must have felt threatened by our half-sized holy man.

Fear and anxiety must have gripped the dead, unbeating heart of the vampire at the mere sight of Brother Fost.

I was unaware that the undead could even experience, let alone feel an emotion like fear.

I was being educated very quickly about the undead by one of their own, and I didn't necessarily want the lessons that were being so graciously offered to me.

Bad news in a small town travels quickly...good news, even quicker...

So it seemed on the morning after the vampire attack.

News of the young girl's rescue and of the fight with the vampire outside the gates of town was thick within 'The Lounge.'

My companions and I sat at our usual table in any tavern we had been to, trying to enjoy our breakfast.

(No coffee for me, as my nerves were already on edge.)

Townsfolk gathered around.

(Most of which had never seen an elf, dwarf or halfling up close before.)

They were asking questions about the night before, thanking us, congratulating us, and simply gawking at the strange newcomers in their town; gossip and whispers filled the room.

We were reluctant to speak, even amongst ourselves; needless to say, we were very uncomfortable.

We quickly finished our meals, thanked our hosts, and left; ten minutes later, we were on our mounts and out on the trail back to Salvus Hus.

We never looked back.

Reflecting on the night before and the events that unfolded, I wondered how different our lives would be if we hadn't stopped, but continued on throughout the night, perhaps stopping to rest in some different location.

My nerves were on fire, the unearthly voice that came from the undead creature that crawled out from some dark, damp, nameless, shallow grave to feast on human blood still rang in my ears… "I'll make you pay with your soul, Ranger!"

The next time we stopped was a few hours later in a clearing in some woods; we set up a simple camp of a cooking fire and began to collect our thoughts.

"The town of Powell would have probably been different on any other occasion," Brother Fost said, breaking the not-so-uncomfortable silence.

"They sure were excited!" Meeka reflected with a slight giggle.

"That vampire attacked the town too quickly after sundown to be random." Sir Quinn observed outwardly, as he tossed a few sticks on the fire.

"Agreed, Knight," Balt grunted, running a sharpening stone over the blade of his Great Axe, "I just wish I'd have had ta chance ta knock that bite'n bastard a good'n b'fore 'e disappeared."

We all sat in silence, apparently in thought about what the two had just said.

(I was, anyway.)

"There's no use dwelling on it now," the knight added abruptly, "it's over and now we should be on our way, back to the castle to report to our King. We must complete our mission."

"After our lunch, Knight," Balt grunted.

"Here, here!" Brother Fost agreed.

Meeka plopped down hard on her butt and folded her arms across her chest in mock defiance.

Loher leaned up against a tree and half smiled.

Sir Quinn just nodded, smiled and tossed the few remaining sticks he still held into the fire.

After a moment, Loher walked to the fire and sat down, "I just can't stop thinking about what that vile monster said as it disappeared."

"An idle threat," I laughed, trying to seem brave, but still not so sure myself.

Meeka nervously giggled with my laugh.

"We stopped it." Several tiny voices unexpectedly sang out in a chorus from nowhere, yet everywhere, "The vampire is gone and it shan't be back."

"What makes ye so sure?" Balt called out, but the only reply he received was the slight rustling of the wind in the leaves.

Brother Fost stood up and walked to Loher, "Loher, my dear, why don't you see if you can scare up a bit of food for us with that mighty bow of yours?"

Loher's half smile widened as she strung up her bow, "It would be my pleasure, are you coming, McLaaud?"

I smiled as well as I gathered up my bow and quiver, and then followed the elven maiden out into the forest.

It didn't take us very long to locate, corner and kill a small deer.

I field dressed the creature with ease, as Loher hunted down and picked a green salad to go along with the meat.

Wild potatoes, strawberries, raspberries, blackberries, blueberries, dandelion greens, wild onions and other assorted salad greens were all put together in a sack to be given to our self-nominated chef.

"Brother Fost is going to be impressed with this magnificent feast," Loher stated with pride, as she helped me sling the deer over my shoulder to carry it back to our camp.

"This should feed us for the next few days." I agreed.

"Not the way Balt eats, and the knight is no picky eater either." Loher laughed, showing the very rare beauty that she so desperately tried to conceal.

It made me wonder why she always tried to keep herself from being happy.

Chapter Six

THE FAIRIES

There comes a time in a person's life when all foolishness must be put aside and the correct questions must be asked...and answered.

What one needs at that very point in time are the correct questions, as well as the correct person to answer them.

I knew I had the correct people before me...

...I just wondered if I knew the correct questions.

———◆———

"The High Priestess of the coven of witches, called The Circle of Flowers, had asked us to keep a good eye on you," a fairie stated.

"It had something to do with that vampire attack last night," another fairie added.

"And sometimes the correct questions don't have to be asked at all," I mumbled.

"What?" Loher asked me.

"Never mind," I answered, lost in a memory of a story of a clown.*

"We have also been asked to have you all join us at the coven's meeting time...err...place... as soon as possible," a completely different fairie added.

"All of your questions will be answered then...err...there," a fourth fairie cut in.

"Will you join us?" Asked a fifth.

"As Loher stated last night, 'We have time to kill.'" Sir Quinn said, "Besides, my curiosity has been piqued."

"We will join you." I finalized.

⁕

Fairie magic is very different than wizard magic, I suppose because it is natural, unlearned.

To be more definitive: with wizard magic such as Meeka's, a verbal incantation must be vocalized, and then there is some sort of obvious visual imagery, such as the thick pinkish smoke as well as some sort of auditory, like a sudden loud pop or poof, just before or during the full execution of such spell, for example: 'Teleportation.'

With fairie magic, the natural variation of magic, it is instant, silent and less visible and much more efficient.

I shared these facts with you, because at one moment, our whole camp including the cooking fire, our mounts, the fairies, my companions and myself were once located hidden within the safety of the grove of trees, and a moment later in the blink of an eye (and just as silent as a blink) we found the whole camp, fire and all, near a lake, out in the open, beside a very large, odd looking well-built brick house.

I have not been everywhere within the Realm of Beornan Heafod, but I am quite sure we were no longer in Beornan Heafod, or anywhere near it anymore.

There was something strange about the way it even felt there, and even the air smelled and tasted different.

Odd, low, powerful noises rumbled from unseen places and it was probably a good thing that we were ushered into the brick dwelling so quickly, because I thought I saw a silverish-grey dragon soaring with spread wings, high, so very high in the sky overhead.

We were being led by a human woman wearing strange, almost tight fitting robes.

She led us through a door and then directly down a flight of wooden stairs and into a dark passage.

My night vision picked up on the cold shapes of oddly shaped crates on shelves.

We were then led through another door and into a large room that was brightly lit, which was quite the opposite of what I had always expected the meeting place for a coven of witches would be like (in my own mind).

The light was emanating from small glass pear-shaped globes, which were covered by cylindrical shades that were narrow at the top and wide at the bottom.

The globes and shades were on wooden stands attached to the wall by long, slim, leash-like contraptions.

The witch's altar was set up in the middle of the room on a large, long rectangular table that was covered in tight green felt.

There were netted holes in each corner of the table, as well as in the center of both long sides, almost as if they were meant to catch something.

At one end of the altar sat a number of solid-colored and striped orbs about the size of an apple, while a pair of slender poles – almost like thin jousting sticks – rested against the altar next to the orbs.

The remainder of the altar was set as I had always imagined a witch's altar would look like, with colored candles, various bowls which held sands and herbs and other unidentifiable reagents, crystal goblets, athames (sacred knives,) stones, tomes, and perhaps a skull or two.

There was even an assortment of large feathers that ranged in colors from black through grey to speckled white.

Strange, enchanting music floated everywhere about the room from an unknown source.

Affixed upon the wall, very near the business end of the altar hung the holy symbol of witches, a five pointed star in a circle; the top point was pointing up, making this recognizable as a pentacle.

(A pentagram is virtually the same symbol, only inverted and is generally recognized as evil, and has no association with the Wiccan religion.)

A half dozen (or more) human men and women stood in a loose group as we were led into the room; the coven members were all wearing strange, slightly similar, almost constricting and very uncomfortable looking clothing.

My companions and I were led to sit in some rather comfortable throne-like chairs as the High Priestess began to speak; the others sat and stood, wide-eyed gawking at us, quite like the townsfolk in Powell.

"We, of the coven 'The Circle of Flowers,' have been trying to keep a close eye on you," the High Priestess began as she walked toward us from the other side of the altar.

"Why us?" I asked, as if coming out of a trance.

The High Priestess smiled and stated, "You have been seen in some of my own clairvoyant visions."

Meeka excitedly spoke up, "Isn't that when you can see the future in a dreamlike state?"

"Correct," the High Priestess answered, still smiling.

"What happens to us in your visions?" Loher demanded.

Suddenly, the High Priestess got a worried look upon her face.

"You might as well tell them, Shannon," a male witch said in a matter-of-a-fact tone, "you **did** bring them here."

The High Priestess, Shannon, shot him an unappreciative look and then reluctantly agreed, "You're right, Jason," she then turned to face us once again, "In my visions, I see one of you turned into a vampire, so I sent my fairies out to protect you."

"That would have been me," I said with an uncomfortable chuckle, "your fairies performed their assignment very well." I complimented.

Shannon and Jason looked at each other with pride in their eyes.

"Pray tell, what would have happened if your fairies had failed?" Loher asked.

"And I had been turned into a vampire?" I finished the question with a shudder.

The High Priestess got a grim look on her face, "My fairies would have attempted to capture you and bring you to that room," she stated and pointed to a door off to the far side of the room behind us.

"What be in there?" Balt growled before I could ask.

"That room holds an airtight, glass chamber which is escape-proof for vampires." Jason offered.

"We have discovered a way to give a willing vampire back its soul," Shannon answered.

"What do you mean, 'willing'?" I asked.

"The vampire must **want** to regain its soul." Shannon answered.

"If I were a vampire, I would most certainly want my soul returned to my body." I said with complete conviction.

I could not imagine myself being a vampire; soulless, undead.

"Well," Jason declared, "that threat has been stopped; the fairies were successful and you don't have to worry about that anymore." He laughed.

"Indeed," Shannon agreed. "We shall now return you to your own..." Her voice trailed off as if in deep thought.

(Your own... time?)

"Realm," Jason completed Shannon's thought for her as our vision switched to...

I opened my eyes. (I think.)

Brother Fost was cooking something that smelled absolutely delicious.

Balt was diligently working away repairing our armor and sharpening our weapons; cleaning off the last battle's gore.

Loher and Meeka were sitting near the fire, chatting among themselves about whatever it is that women chat about, while Sir Quinn was busy feeding and watering our mounts.

Were we really there with the coven of witches?

It seemed a bit later in the day, was it all just a crazy dream?

I noticed I was sitting comfortably on the ground in a faint but warm ray of sunlight, leaning up against a large oak.

Slowly, I got up to my feet, yet I still felt a bit groggy.

Loher looked over at me and flashed me one of her rare and beautiful smiles, "Did you have a nice rest?" She asked, "You weren't asleep for very long."

"I..." I began, but then involuntarily stretched, my back reported with a loud pop.

A fairie quickly zipped past my head with a high pitched laugh.

I felt a light tap on my cheek – another fairie, on my shoulder.

I quickly took a look around, trying to focus my eyes, and I spotted two more fairies sitting together on a low branch of a birch tree.

I shook my head; still trying to fully wake up, "Were we—" I began.

"Yes," Loher said, the campfire reflected in her purple violet eyes, "You said you were sleepy, so you lay down in that sunspot against that tree to take a nap as soon as we..." She paused, trying to grasp the correct term.

"Returned to this realm," the fairie on my shoulder completed.

"Perhaps 'time' would be the correct term," one of the fairies in the birch suggested.

"Let us not confuse the poor ranger," the fairie's partner scolded, "he has been through enough."

"Yes, Dear," the first fairie submitted.

My stomach abruptly growled, "I'm starving!" I conveyed, "What's cooking?"

"Rabbit," Brother Fost announced.

I almost lost my appetite.

After lunch, we mounted our horses and continued on our way to the Royal city of Salvus Hus.

Once again, as we traveled, we reflected upon the experiences we just went through, like our trip to meet the witches of the coven called The Circle of Flowers, and the information on the discovery of reuniting a willing vampire with its soul.

"How long have you been watching us?" I asked the fairies as they flew around at my side.

"Do you remember the rabbit race?" A fairie asked as it brushed past my ear.

My meal turned over and churned violently in my guts, and I began to feel a bit sick. "Yes," I answered sourly, "my mind flashes back to that moment quite often, thank you."

"We began to follow you just before then," a fairie sang.

"We followed the Royal Messenger all the way to your home," another fairie near Meeka giggled, reflecting the wizard's personality.

Our party continued along on our course talking, joking and telling stories of our various pasts; the fairies even sang a traditional song of their own people that was so strikingly beautiful and harmonious that Meeka actually began to cry.

"That was only six of us singing," One of the fairies admitted, "you all should hear that song being sung by a whole traditional choir of a thousand or more!"

"Perhaps some time in the future we will," Meeka sniffled as she dried her eyes and smiled.

"I'm afraid the time has come, my friends." The lead fairie that was perched upon Balt's helm announced.

"Ta time fer wot?" Balt queried.

"The time for us to leave you," another fairie giggled, "now that the vampire has moved on."

"Hold on a minute," Loher countered nervously, "that vampire **swore** it would come back!"

"I'll make you pay with your soul, Ranger!" I quoted.

There was a sharp laugh, "I will still be around!" Brendt called from a cruising altitude high above our heads.

"Wot guid be ye, Sprite?" Balt grumbled impatiently, "Yer na immune te a vampire's bite any more'n we are, ye said so yerself!"

"We have a natural communication link with sprites," the lead fairie on Balt's helm explained.

"We can be here in a literal blink of an eye if we need to be," another said.

"I plan to keep well out of the way!" Brendt stammered with a slightly nervous laugh.

"Trust us, if you don't yet," two more fairies sang out as a chime.

"We have no choice but to trust you, our new friends." I agreed.

Sir Quinn and Loher gave agreeing looks in my direction.

Brother Fost still looked a bit nervous and Balt was too busy dodging low flying fairies to comment.

It seemed as if they were bombarding the poor dwarf as a sort of fun game; the dwarven warrior was not the slightest bit amused.

"Then it is settled," the lead fairie announced, as she took graceful flight from her place on Balt's head, "We will stay in contact with our cousin Brendt and return in the event of an undead emergency."

"Many thanks to you and yours, dear fairies," I offered and raised my hand in a friendly salute.

Our mounts trotted on as the fairies quickly vanished from sight, one by one.

CHAPTER SEVEN
SALVUS HUS

The sun was just peeking over the horizon as we arrived at North Ferian Harbor.

There were several boats and ships docked along the pier, as well as one very familiar ship, The Scorpion.

"Isna tat ta ship wot took us—" Balt began.

"—It is!" Meeka exclaimed excitedly, cutting the dwarf's words off completely.

The Scorpion's captain noticed we were there as well and began to wave in our direction.

We began waving back as well, too far away to make any vocal communication.

Our party boarded the ferry to North Port Royale, anxious to report back to the young King.

We had a lot of information for him, and we wondered what his reaction, if any, would be.

The young King was sometimes difficult to read, according to Sir Quinn and Brother Fost.

The morning had begun to turn into a beautiful day, with a light, pleasant breeze that carried the fragrance of wildflowers and ripe berries.

Seagulls played their noisy chasing games high above our heads, while the waters below were so calm and clear that I could see not only big fish, but huge monster fish swimming seemingly along with the ferry.

The trip across the water was so calming and peaceful that at that very moment in time, I had forgotten all about the not-so-pleasant encounters from our recent journey that would soon reside within our pasts.

I had made some new friends on this adventure that I hoped to keep lifelong.

"What are you going to do after this, McLaaud?" Loher asked, snapping me out of my thoughts and back to the ferry.

I stood there for a moment, gazing into her purple-violet eyes, wondering what was going on behind them. "I guess that depends on what the King says," I answered, "What about you? What will you do?"

She laughed and then answered, "It depends on what the King says." She stood there gazing distantly across the water.

Behind us, I could hear Balt and Brendt arguing about something trivial.

It made me laugh to think that perhaps the sprite did such things to the dwarf on purpose, just to get a jovial rise out of the poor fighter.

The ferry finally docked at North Port Royale and we took our mounts across to dry land.

Once again, both the portman and the ferryman refused payment; we were soon on the trail, a stack of coins secretly left behind on a rail near the draw plank of the ferry.

As we began to lead our mounts away, we heard a sharp whistle from the water's edge.

I quickly turned around and saw The Scorpion anchored just off shore with the captain standing on the deck waving us down, "What'cha dooin' all de wey over de'ar, Mon?" The captain asked, yelling across the distance with his hands cupped around his mouth.

Sir Quinn called back, "We have to report back to our King!"

"Well den," the captain called back, "Me be meet'n ya at de castle when me gets de'ar!"

"I guess we'll see you there!" The knight called back and then turned back to the trail.

"Aren't we going to wait for him?" Brother Fost innocently asked.

"We could," Sir Quinn answered with a pause, "But I think it's better if we continue on ahead. Besides, I'm sure he has a lot of work to do beforehand, and I for one am very anxious to get home, aren't you?"

"Aye, Knight." Balt answered for Brother Fost, "I c'n 'ear a pint o' ale jest a callin' me name out, Laddy."

"I'll agree with that, Master Dwarf!" I laughed, lightly nudging Stahvee into motion.

A moment or so later, with Sir Quinn at point, the gate guards waved us through with no questions asked.

(The Royal badges on our tunics actually made all of the difference.)

The stable owner, Festus, greeted us with warm delight as we stored our mounts within his trusted care.

Sir Quinn bid us all a fond farewell until later as he disappeared beyond the castle walls, Brother Fost quietly retired to his room in the abbey while Meeka... No one really knows where Meeka literally disappeared to in a puff of pink smoke.

Brendt vanished as well.

Balt, Loher and I found ourselves in 'The Broken Blade,' having a well-deserved meal and some eagerly welcomed drinks; and yes... we **did** sit in our usual seats, like the creatures of habit we are.

⸺◆⸺

The food was filling and delicious, the drinks were strong and smooth, and the company—

Well, the company was unlike it had ever been before; enjoying drinks with those that alcohol does not affect the way it does a human was a joy I rarely had the honor to experience, although it affected me only half as much as it did the typical human, as I am only half human.

Being half human, half of my family is human and they always seemed to be around, so this indeed was a very rare occasion.

The dwarf had become quite laid back and the she-elf was finally showing just the right amount of kind-hearted emotion.

(Elves are not emotionally impaired, but Loher seemed to be, most of the time.)

Then there was me—I laughed a lot and no one seemed to mind in the slightest, as a matter of a fact, Balt even laughed a bit more whenever I would start in, which would make me laugh even harder.

Balt seemed to have had a good time because at the end of the night, even he, a dwarf, was staggering to his room.

The next thing I remember was waking up the next morning in my room with Loher sitting near me on the edge of my bed.

She was sitting there, looking- no- staring out the window at the rising sun in a deep unblinking gaze; she was 'sleeping' in her meditative state that she would later describe as her 'reverie'.

I moved my foot and she instantly snapped back into a conscious state of alertness.

"Were you sitting there all night?" I calmly asked her.

"Yes," she answered, "is that alright?"

"Ummm... yeah, I guess—" I began.

"—I don't see the point of getting my own room because I rarely, if ever, sleep." She said cutting me off.

"I don't mind." I said, finishing my statement.

"I have some other reasons for picking your room as well, if you would care to hear them," she offered.

"By all means," I said, intrigued.

"For one, Meeka snores, but more importantly, besides the fact that we are both of elven blood, and when I **do** decide to actually lay down and **sleep** – I prefer **not** to do it **alone... And**, I picked you because I can protect you better in case that vampire decides to make good on its promise to 'make you pay with your soul... Ranger,'" she said all in one easy breath.

I simply smiled.

"Now, if you would not mind getting up, I would like to go down to 'The Blade' and have some breakfast, and I'm quite sure you could use some of..." She thought for a moment and then asked, "What was that drink called?"

"Coffee," I answered, "and yes, actually, I would love some."

I got out of bed, quickly got dressed and strapped on my gear, and as we were walking out the door I asked, "When you **do** sleep—"

"—Later," she shot, cutting me off once again, this time with a stern but playful look.

When Loher and I arrived, the rest of the team, including our friend, the captain of The Scorpion, Captain Mario Waxx, were there drinking coffee and some were eating breakfast.

"G'marnin'!" Balt said in a cheerful tone and raised his mug of... whatever it was that he was drinking, as the two of us sat down with our coffee; Loher had a plate of breakfast as well.

I raised my mug of coffee and met Balt's, yawning as I did so; Balt gave out a good chuckle.

Sir Quinn gave me a (secret) 'look' as if to say, "Did you two...?"

I slightly, but effectively, shook my head as if to say, "No."

The knight simply shrugged his shoulders as if to say, "Better luck next time."

I shook my head as if to say, "Shut up."

Loher looked up, unaware of our (secret) voiceless conversation.

Sir Quinn and I stopped 'talking.'

Balt smiled.

I took a short pull from my coffee and then finally asked, "When will we see the King?"

"De King be expectin' us shartly, Mon." Captain Waxx announced and took a long pull from his own drink – an ale, I believe.

"Did the King send for you as well?" Brother Fost asked Captain Waxx.

"I asked if he would join us when we were on our way back from the cave." Sir Quinn answered before Waxx had the chance.

Brother Fost nodded his understanding.

"I be wait'n de'ar down by de port for all –a two days, Mon," the captain laughed with a smile. "No worries though, t'was nice. Relax'n." He took another giant gulp of his drink.

———◦———

We finished up with breakfast and then slowly made our way to the castle's main doors.

"He's with us." Sir Quinn announced to the guards regarding Captain Waxx as we passed.

"Just do as we do and you'll be fine," Brother Fost assured the captain, "The King dislikes the usual formalities."

"No worries," the captain habitually commented.

The young ruler of the Realm of Beornan Heafod sat upon his lonely throne, looking bored as we casually strolled up the vibrant red carpet and stood before him.

The captain of The Scorpion bowed low and then looked around in confusion and slight embarrassment when he noticed that the rest of us had not done the same.

Both the King and the wizard let out a playful giggle.

I smiled at the captain and the King rolled his eyes. "Welcome back, my friends," the young King said as he stood up, "Who is our new dark skinned friend?"

"Tis be Cap'n Mario Waxx, yer Highness... oops, sorry." Balt apologized at the unwanted formality, but the King waved it off as alright. "He be ta cap'n o' ta ship called Ta Scorpion."

"I hired him," Sir Quinn announced, "for our personal transportation needs."

"Very good, Sir Knight," the King agreed.

"I took dem to de new cave, yer Hi—" The captain stopped himself. Meeka giggled again.

"Ahh, the new cave," the young King said, now quite interested. "Please tell me about the new cave, my friends!"

We all just stood there in silence looking at each other, trying to determine who would begin, then, as if by some mystic calling, we each told a part of the adventure, one by one with flawless cooperation, to its completion.

Lagu Ofer'Eal had an amused look upon his young face as he tried to absorb the information as efficiently as humanly possible.

He had asked us to revisit certain parts of the 'meat' of our quest within the cave itself, although he especially enjoyed the part with my flashback on the ship for some reason.

He laughed about it... I found this both odd and slightly disturbing.

The vampire sequence scared him a bit, especially because the vampire is reported as 'at large,' which compelled him to inform us that he was going to hire a professional vampire hunter at once... and he did; he called in a messenger and ordered it to be done.

After hearing the whole adventure once again from other points of view, (which we all agreed was a very wise course of action,) he had asked us to retire for the day and return to him around noon the next day.

(He was still a kid and apparently wanted to sleep in late.)

Some of us went for a walk around the grounds and then returned to our respective rooms, while others just simply retired for the night without a walk.

Loher decided to join me in my room once again; she did not sleep.

We returned the next day at noon, as ordered, and the young King met us all out in the courtyard.

We casually strolled around the Royal grounds within the castle gates for a while, talking and retelling the events of the journey.

As we reached the gates again, after a second go-round of the castle grounds, the young King strapped on the signature sword of the Royal Family, called 'The Burning Blade' which was not an actual flaming sword, nor did it heat up or cauterize the wounds it so easily inflicted.

In fact, it had absolutely no magical properties or enhancements at all; it was just simply an ornately crafted, fancy looking sword with an extremely sharp and well-kept blade.

(Shhh!!! - Don't tell a soul!)

The King himself was adorned in exquisite attire, including the crown, which he rarely wore.

We walked through the gates and out among the peasants on the common streets of Salvus Hus.

He was obviously embarrassed and uncomfortable as his people stopped in their tracks and stared – star-struck and rightfully so.

Most people dropped to their knees where they stood, some bent into outrageously low bows in honor of their King.

We slowly walked to the center of town to where the gallows pole was located, and the young King stood where the executioner would stand where everyone could see him; he raised his hands high above his head...

"My people!" He called loudly.

The town hushed.

"My good people of Beornan Heafod!" He called again, louder and then waited.

People began gathering around, literally crawling out of the woodwork and from every nook and cranny possible, just to hear the words of their young ruler.

"My good people let my words be heard from the Mons to the Wudu and everywhere in between and far away!" The King paused.

"In one week, that is seven days... in one week's time I must have an army..."

"...I must have **MY Army!!**" He cried loud enough that his still developing voice cracked and pitched sharply.

The people of Salvus Hus cheered and scattered off in every direction to quickly spread the word of the young King's command.

Within days, people from all walks of life and almost every race, began to gather in Salvus Hus.

Knights, guards, ex-guards and Royal Soldiers also made their way back to those beloved castle gates in order to serve their King once again.

After the first five days, men and goodish creature alike were either accepted or respectfully turned away.

Exactly one week to the very hour of his announcement, the young King walked the ranks of his new army.

Out of over three-thousand men and humanoid creatures that had arrived at the castle gates to report to serve, only a mere fifty able bodies were chosen.

These fifty soldiers were handpicked by a team of commanders that consisted of: five of the six of us companions (Brother Fost excluded himself for his own personal reasons), as well as Captain Waxx, the captain of the Royal Guards, and the commander of the Royal Army, who has served in the Royal Army and worked his way up the ranks since the age of fifteen.

Fifty soldiers...

The best of the best...

Men, elves, dwarves and even a few trusted orcs that had once served as Royal Soldiers before, made up our army that would be going back into the new cave.

The mission:

Sweep and clear the new cave of any and all non-goodish creatures, and map out the entire area on the way through.

Or, in other words...

Seek out and destroy anything that does not choose to serve the King and make sure to map out the entire area, so no one gets lost in there in the future.

The King addressed the training team which consisted of: Sir Quinn, teaching the virtues of honor, loyalty and bravery;

The commander of the Royal Army, teaching the basic fighting skills;

Balt, teaching advanced fighting techniques;

Meeka, teaching those who could use magic;

And finally when all were trained in the aforementioned skills, everyone was sent to Loher to learn the valuable and necessary art of archery...

..."I want you all to take as much time as you need," the young King began, "to teach and train this army the skills they will need to successfully carry out this mission and come back alive."

With that order given, the training team gathered up the fifty soldiers and began the grueling process of turning ordinary fighters into multi-skilled warriors, as well as turning novice casters of parlor tricks into powerful wizards of sorts.

Each soldier would then be equipped with a blade and a bow.

—◆—

Approximately two months later, fifty-eight of us marched from the gates of Salvus Hus to the docks of North Port Royale, where The Scorpion waited, anchored just off shore.

As we marched toward the port, the portman's eyes went from wide and excited, to sad and disappointed when he saw us slowly boarding The Scorpion, not his ferry; he could have almost felt the weight of our coins in his purse, although he would have of course, refused any payment from a Royal Party, knowing full well that we would have left some coins behind.

Two-hundred-sixty 'men' set sail on The Scorpion from North Port Royale, north to the Strait of Avilyn.

From there, The Scorpion turned northeast and sailed to the island region just east of the Ferrum Mons, called The Haze Cove.

The Scorpion sailed into The Haze and turned southeast past the Yfel Holh Caves (sounds like "E-Fell Hole Caves" which actually translates to "Evil Hollow Caves.") and then swung north to retrace the once followed path to the new cave.

The whole trip by sea took just under a week, but in detail, the trip was more like...

Day One:

The Scorpion pulled away from the northern dock at first light.

The waters were calm and the sun was just barely peeking over the Mons.

Captain Waxx was calling out the final orders for departure and the crew was hustling about, carrying out those given orders.

Meeka was taking in the beauty of the surrounding nature as it all slowly awoke from its silent slumber.

Sir Quinn was going over the route we were to take with the ship's helmsman and navigator.

Balt was admiring the ship's cannons and harpoon systems, while Brother Fost was cursing himself for eating a big breakfast after being warned that it would probably be better if he did not eat at all.

(At least for the first day.)

Loher and I stood on the deck and watched our progression; the elven maiden seemed oddly stuck to my side lately, and I was not sure how to react.

She seemed wary of the sailors and soldiers, yet I was reluctant to believe that she was afraid; although I may have been mistaken... stranger things have happened.

Midday:

Things were fairly calm, the sun was brightly shining as the soldiers were trying to concentrate on their training with the commander, but having a difficult time of it, because Meeka was wearing next to nothing and lying on the deck, soaking up the rays of the sun.

Sir Quinn was observing the soldiers' training while secretly gazing upon the beautiful wizard's recreational activity.

Balt was explaining some advanced battle techniques to some other soldiers, while Brother Fost was fishing with some of the sailors.

Loher had slightly eased away from me, yet still kept me well within visual range while she lazily gazed off into the distance.

There wasn't really much to see, other than the occasional peek through the trees at a meadow, perhaps the edge of Hydan Seir; we **were** near the Xobish battle ground.

I kept a weather eye.

Evening:

The dimming light brought out a whole lot of stars in the clear night sky, as well as a few waves, as we reached the northern portion of the river.

Everyone was resting, except Sir Quinn, Captain Waxx, the on-duty crew and needless to say, the elves; we were about to exit the river and spill out into the Strait of Avilyn.

Avilyn—

Now **there's** a name of interest...

There are many, many myths and legends about Avilyn, the king of the dragons, most of which are assumed untrue.

Out of all of the true stories I know for sure, my favorite one has got to be of how the Dead Desert Dunelands, located on the northern island portion of the realm, were created...

...The shortened version of the story began, as I have already told you earlier on in our tale, as the dragons' solution to the ever-going battle between the forces of good and evil; hence dubbing this Realm the name of 'Beornan Heafod' – 'Burning Head'.

As the lesser dragons of the realm swept over and cleared the mainland of the lesser battles, the dragon king, Avilyn, looked down from high above and witnessed the largest of the battles, the battle between mortal foes: the hill giants and the now extinct race, the cyclops.

As legend states:

Where the Dead Desert Dunelands sit now, the hill giant/cyclops battle raged on for centuries.

The dragon king chose this area to cleanse, leaving the rest of the realm for the lesser dragons.

In the time it took the lesser dragons to cleanse the mainland, Avilyn had used each and every one of his breath types, ranging from a simple fire cone, to an ice storm, as well as a giant acid cloud, a powerful web of lightning bursts and everything in between.

He concentrated these breath weapons on the most northern island, turning it from a lush green, foliage covered land, to the dead sandy wastelands you see there today, destroyed forever, left barren, devoid of life...

...So the story goes.

Day Two:

The sun rose over the Strait of Avilyn, revealing The Scorpion sailing east towards the Mons and beyond.

It would take us until sundown to reach Avilyn Harbor because we were sailing against the wind, making progress slower than wanted.

Now, in open sea, the water had become a bit choppy, which some of the passengers were not used to and of my companions (besides the elves and the on-duty crew,) I was the only one awake.

Sir Quinn and Balt arose shortly before breakfast was served; Balt ate and then went directly back to sleep.

He would later admit that the rocking motion of the ship on the water lulled him back into peaceful sleep.

Midday:

Something bumped into the ship!

Not just a simple tap, but a fully-fledged, heartfelt **bump.**

The Scorpion had traveled this exact route many, many times and Captain Waxx knew for certain that there were no rocks or reef just below the water's surface.

This, whatever it was, had been something big...

Something alive...

Something - mobile.

As a precaution, the sailors and soldiers were put on full alert and Meeka had started to chant some sort of memorized spell, as a 'shield.'

The very air around the ship began to wave and crackle – actually throb with a heightened energy level.

Sir Quinn stood up top in the look-out-tower, called the 'Crow's Nest' to keep watch for some sort of danger from below, but saw nothing.

Balt had taken up a position at one of the ship's harpoon guns, while Brother Fost somehow managed to sleep through the whole thing.

Loher and I stood poised, back to back with our bows at the ready and waited.

Two hours and no bumps later, an "All Clear" was announced and most of us began to relax.

Evening:

Brought much discussion of sea monsters and other such myths, legends and stories of the sea.

The subject of pirates also came up, but was quickly dismissed as taboo, well before it even had a chance to begin; some of the crew, including the captain, seemed a bit edgy at the mere mention of the subject.

Night Time:

Slowly the conversations came to a close as the twinkling stars began to show brightly in the still clear night sky.

The 'Skeleton Crew' took over the duties as the rest of us found our bunks.

Day Three:

Sun-up; still sailing against the wind as Avilyn Harbor was now behind us, passed by in the very wee hours of the morning.

Off to our right, we could now see the Ferrum Mons looming up ahead; we would be passing the dwarven homelands and turning south, just before sunset.

The water had become a bit choppier still and patches of clouds had begun to molest the sun.

The crew had begun their preparations for the southbound turn, while the soldiers continued their vigilant watch for danger, now in shifts.

After breakfast, Meeka sat down with her tome opened before her, studying intently, barely ever looking up to take any sort of break.

Sir Quinn stayed busy studying the map.

Balt took (loving) care of all of the weapons and armor he could gather, including those of our party.

Brother Fost stayed down below deck; I'm not sure what it was that he had been doing this whole time down there, as I had barely even seen him.

Loher and her archers practiced close quarters combat techniques with their bows, which proved to be quite effective against humanoid foes.

And as for myself, I stayed up in the 'Crow's Nest' to keep watch on both the weather and the as-of-yet-unseen creature situation...If there even was one.

Midday:

The Ferrum Mons was now just directly to our right, or "Off the starboard bow," as the helmsman announced, and there were also mountains off to our left, or "Port," as well – **far** off to our left.

The Haze was directly ahead.

The soldiers were once again put on high alert as "A very large creature of unknown origin," according to Sir Quinn, who was stationed in the 'Crow's Nest,' "almost surfaced off to the left, yet it did not break through the surface of the water itself!"

The creature had created quite the stir among the ranks as they were now extremely anxious to engage 'The Beast' in combat.

Night:

The word "Illuminare!" had become a common sound aboard The Scorpion.

Bright flashes of light pulsed here and there among the decks of the ship as Meeka's students practiced their 'light' spells.

Constant attention was being paid to the water surrounding the ship, yet no creature contact was made that night; it is my belief that the flashing of the 'light' spells kept the creature at bay.

Day Four:

In The Haze, heading south, the morning hours produced no sign of the creature below the waves, regardless, a constant high alert was kept in place on deck as well as in the 'Crow's Nest.'

Midday:

No sign of the creature, but a 'Crow's Nest' call reported an unidentified ship off the port bow flying no colors... possibly smugglers or pirates.

We maintained a safe distance and after a few hours, the unknown ship had vanished over the horizon; that evening and night were uneventful.

Day Five:

Still uneventful, besides our turn to the north, but by Midday, the Yfel Holh Caves were off to our left, and then another hour later the new cave was in sight.

A hearty cheer rose up among the ranks.

That night, until the early morning hours of the next day, two elaborate camps were erected; one on the island and one still aboard The Scorpion.

Songs and stories of adventure and fortune, danger and fame rang out from between the two camps.

Entry plans were discussed and made:

Sir Quinn, the commander (Vlad) and I agreed upon...

Two waves of soldiers, twenty-five in each wave, will be separately sent in only after the scout team, consisting of the original six members: Sir Quinn, Balt, Loher, Meeka, Brother Fost and I, enter and secure the area of any immediate threat.

Sir Quinn will come back out to signal and lead the first wave of soldiers and then an hour or so later, Commander Vlad will enter the cave leading the second wave of soldiers.

Hopefully, by that time, either the scout team, led by me or the first wave of soldiers will have established contact with Bolla, the lacerta holy man and perhaps a team of his own soldiers.

A base camp within the cave will be set up as well.

Depending on how large Bolla's team is, if he even has one, small 'units' of soldiers will be sent in waves from the centralized base camp to sweep, clear and map the caverns and tunnels.

If by chance Bolla does not have a team, or he is not contacted, smaller waves of soldiers will take the place of the afore stated 'units.'

After an entire section of the area has been cleared and mapped, the base camp will then move to a deeper location within the cave, leaving a satellite camp in its place; the process will continue until the entire cave has been charted.

Each 'unit' will consist of an undetermined number of soldiers, archers, mappers and a magic-using chaperone.

The number of each type of person will ultimately depend on if Bolla is contacted and has a team with him.

Night:

The starry sky was a brilliant shimmering meadow of twinkling lights that seemed to reach on and on into the heavens.

I have to admit that I was feeling a bit nervous about our task that we had to perform starting early the next morning; the creatures known as the olyame were my main concern.

Sleep was not an option, yet it was sorely sought.

Loher stuck close by my side, and I was beginning to enjoy her company more than I had before, although I was sure that she had ulterior motives for being so close and could not have the same budding feelings that I was developing for her.

Food, drink and friendship were passed from campfire to campfire as the night moved forward, with no intentions of stopping until the sun would show up to chase it back to its dark and humble abode.

Songs and stories were heard well into the night, as each and every one of us surely prayed to his or her own God(dess) for strength and bravery, and the ability to survive the trials we most certainly would face within the approaching hours.

CHAPTER EIGHT
THE CAVE

The fifty-some member Royal Army was assembled into two teams and stood waiting, anxious.

As the sun's first rays shattered the darkness like a thin sheet of glass, it was time!

Stealthily, I led the scout team up the face of the mountain and back in through the mouth of the new cave.

There was no real need to be that quiet, so as we made our way to the first fork, where we had met the lacerta, we chose to cast our stealth aside with a nervous little laugh.

The raging river could already be heard in the distance, so far down below.

"Care to toss a coin this time, Brother Fost?" I teased as we approached the place we had stopped before.

"I don't mind if I do!" The priest said, surprisingly, as he plucked a copper coin from his purse and gave it a little flick, so it spun down as it fell toward the surface below. – 'Tiiiinnnngggggg!'

Meeka giggled as she tried to follow the coin with her gaze.

(...We counted until we heard it hit bottom...)

...We never heard it hit.

(Déjà Vu)

"Where'd ye wanna set up ta base camp?" Balt finally asked after the several wasted minutes of foolishness.

"I suggest that we sweep the room where Brother Fost found the runes first, and then, if we don't make that room the base ca—" I began, but Sir Quinn rudely cut me off...

"Not a very good idea to make that room the base camp," the knight countered.

"Why not?" I asked, quite annoyed.

"If we were to be attacked, we would have no escape route," the knight answered.

"Aye," Balt half agreed with a laugh, "ta knight 'as a guid point.'"

"I think that we should set up the base camp down where our tour ended the last time we were here," Loher suggested.

After a moment, we all agreed with the elven maiden's suggestion and then continued walking down the path, keeping an eye out for fresh tracks and markings.

We finally arrived at the fork, the place that we first met the lacerta holy man, Bolla.

The faint smell of acrid smoke, from the burning reptilian corpses a few months ago, was still hanging in the damp cavern air; it made me feel a bit sick to my stomach.

I motioned Meeka and Balt to follow me into the tunnel.

"Illuminare!" Meeka whispered as her 'light' spell illuminated the curving tunnel before us.

"Try to stay between us," I suggested to her as we began to head deeper down the now brightly lit tunnel.

We went in ten feet and then stopped – no new tracks, no sound.

We continued in for another ten feet and then checked for tracks again – nothing and still no sounds at all.

We made it as far as thirty feet and then stopped to check for tracks again – no tracks, but what was that—?

"What ye be 'fraid 'o, Mate?" Balt asked with a chuckle, as he stepped past Meeka and lightly nudged me from behind.

I whipped around and gave him an ice-cold gaze that made both the dwarf and the wizard stop dead in their tracks.

Balt's face went ash white as the sound grew loud enough for him to hear.

I knew that they had both heard it because the usual bubbly look on Meeka's face suddenly turned to a look of sheer terror as the sound grew louder.

"What **is** that?" Meeka asked.

"T'aint no olyame," Balt shivered.

The sound, which was moving closer from in front of us, was growing steadily louder, as whatever it was that was creating the sound drew closer to us as well.

It sounded like a slow, sloshing - wet noise, almost as if someone or some**thing** was pushing a bag of thin, gooey material, end-over-end down the tunnel before us.

"Back up, back up, back up, Lass!" Balt whispered excitedly, as he began to retreat.

(Balt? – Retreat?)

I quickly followed with absolutely no argument at all.

If the realm's bravest and toughest dwarven fighter had decided to retreat, well, then so was I!

Meeka didn't hesitate either, she turned tail quickly and bolted down the tunnel, her 'light' spell followed right along behind her.

The sound continued toward us at its same steady pace.

Those same thirty feet that we had just covered on the way in, seemed more like three-hundred feet on the way out.

As we spilled out of the mouth of the tunnel, we must have had horrified looks upon all of our faces, because as soon as I regained my composure and got back to my feet, I noticed that the whole team had their weapons at the ready and stood waiting with their eyes as wide as full moons, focused upon the tunnel's mouth.

(Slosh, slosh...)

Brother Fost looked at Balt and then at the mouth of the tunnel, back at Balt and then at me, he then looked back at the mouth of the tunnel and then finally back at Balt, "Wh...whah...what ih...**is** that?" The halfling stuttered as a horrified look pitched camp on his face and decided it was so nice there; it might just stay for a while.

"We're not sure, Broth—" Meeka began, but a loud gurgling sound erupted from the tunnel and drowned out the rest of her words.

Then... silence.

A few moments passed before the sloshing wet bag sound continued at a faster pace and came closer and closer still.

(Slosh, slosh...)

The sound was maddening...

(Slosh, slosh...)

Then, finally, it appeared from the mouth of the tunnel.

At first it just looked like a few squid-like tentacles squirming and groping their way through the tunnel's opening, but as the sucker covered arms grew longer, a grotesque shape emerged out after them.

The... **thing's** body looked like that of a giant, rear facing rat, only hairless, veiny and transparent.

The tentacles protruded out of the creature like a dozen tails that pulled it through the tunnel backwards, and the sloshing sound was made as the rat-like shaped liquid filled body would more or less slide and slosh lazily behind.

(It was a rather disgusting and gruesome spectacle to observe.)

"The riza?" Loher asked, disgusted.

"Ta wot?" Balt countered.

"Riza," I echoed, "Cousins of the mer'folk, no, it's not a riza."

"How do you know, McLaaud?" The elven maiden asked.

"The riza cannot breathe in the open air like the mer'folk can, Loher, remember what Bolla told us?" I reflected.

"No," she answered, "but I'll believe you."

The rest of our companions uttered their agreements as we stood there in slightly hypnotized terror.

The creature abruptly stopped, raised its rat-like portion up into the air and began making that terrible loud gurgling sound again; the rat-like end began to violently shake.

Then... unexpectedly ... in a burning flash...

...The creature was engulfed in bright yellow and blue flames mere moments later.

Flaming arrows had silently soared over our hypnotized heads and buried themselves into the soft flesh of the horrible squid-like-rat creature.

We quickly whipped around to see a large group of lacerta archers standing behind us on the ledge path beyond the fork that we were standing at.

Their leader was a familiar soul to see; Bolla, the lacerta holy man whom we had captured and then decided to trust mere months before in the room we were just attempting to re-search.

Bolla stepped closer and tossed a copper coin to our halfling priest, "Lose something?" he hissed, perhaps with a lizard-like smile... we couldn't tell.

Sir Quinn thanked Bolla and his archers and then departed, back to the mouth of the new cave to get wave one of the Royal Soldiers.

"What **was** that... **thing**, your archers just killed?" I asked, as I shook Bolla's... hand? (Claw?)

"That, my friends, was a Rackarn," Bolla answered.

"Rackarn?" Meeka echoed.

"Right," Bolla chuckled, "very dangerous. They hypnotize their pray by—" Bolla's sentence was suddenly drowned out and everyone's attention was shifted to the sound of marching feet, as wave one of the Royal Army noisily ebbed into the cave and began its slow approach.

"We still have to check out that room!" Loher said, trying to talk over the sound of the marching army.

"Agreed," I...agreed, and then said, "let's just hope there are no more of those rackarn in there."

"There shouldn't be," Bolla offered, "my guess is, that there is nothing left alive in that room and you're lucky you got out of there when you did. Rackarn generally travel alone and efficiently kill and consume anything, well, almost anything they come into contact with."

"I guess that's a good thing," I said as I grabbed Loher's arm and called for Meeka and Balt to join us.

"You four go right on ahead," Brother Fost chuckled, relieved that he was not included in the group, "I'm sure Bolla and I have some 'holy talk' we can attend to."

"Illuminare!" Meeka loudly conjured as we passed through the mouth of the tunnel.

The wizard then produced a scrap of parchment and a stick of charcoal, and began to map out the tunnel and the room, once we arrived into it.

As Bolla had foreseen, the room was quite empty and nothing had changed for the last few months... other than the charred bodies of the dead lacerta now being gone, consumed by the rackarn.

Satisfied, we returned to our friends at the fork.

By the time we appeared from the mouth of the tunnel, Sir Quinn and the first wave of the Royal Army had arrived at the fork to meet us.

We also noticed that a few more lacerta, warriors this time, had joined the group during our absence.

These lacerta newcomers wielded swords and shields and some donned helms upon their heads, they all looked a bit more muscular than their bow wielding counterparts; my scouting team and I were pleasantly surprised to see the extra lacerta.

The leader of the lacerta warriors bowed low to me and then offered his... hand-type appendage. (Claw?)

"My name is Ollie," he announced as I shook his...hand.

Bolla shrugged and rolled his eyes, "My youngest brother," he chuckled.

My team and I bowed and introduced ourselves in return.

"I have fifteen more well-trained warriors waiting below," Ollie boasted.

"Well, that's very good to know," Sir Quinn said hurriedly, as he ushered us down the path. "Perhaps we should join them. I trust you already have this area of the cave mapped."

"What be yer hurry, Knight?" Balt growled roughly as he took a step forward to intercept the knight.

Sir Quinn had an extremely anxious look on his face and then, realizing what his haste looked like, he relaxed, eased off and explained, "Friends, 'wave two' is about to move in here, and I suggest we take 'wave one' and move before we cause unneeded congestion here on this path. We **must** stick to the plans."

"Right," Brother Fost agreed as Balt backed off, in silent agreement as well.

We continued down the narrow ledge-path, winding our way towards the bottom as several mappers tracked and sketched our progress and route.

Those maps will then be closely compared by a 'master mapper,' and then finally transferred onto a large 'master map' for the King's record.

We could already hear 'wave two' of the Royal Army enter the mouth of the new cave as we finally arrived at the bottom, where our tour ended the last time we were here.

The combined cacophony of the marching soldiers and the rushing water of the river made it almost impossible to hear any approaching danger.

A group of mappers led by Brother Fost immediately began setting up the base camp/command center, as other mappers stepped in and began to map out the surrounding area; each mapper was armed, as well as escorted by a group of soldiers, archers and a magic user.

Lines of other archers stood ready at all times, covering the mapping groups as well as the groups of soldiers that stood waiting, in case of an attack.

As we arrived, the fifteen lacerta warriors that were stationed there below were just finishing up with an olyame attack; the archers that were along with us jumped in and helped out their sword wielding counterparts.

Score Board: Lacerta: 4 – Olyame: 0.

Ollie led a young but large lacerta warrior to my team and I, "This is my son, Drez," Ollie said as Drez bowed low to us. "Drez will be leading one of our lacerta attachments, assisting in the mapping as my father and I will lead our own attachments, assisting the sweep and clear forces."

"Very good," I agreed, "we welcome your assistance."

The two lacerta bowed again and then blended back into the army.

The sounds of the marching had overpowered the sound of the raging river as 'wave two' of the Royal Army flowed down the narrow ledge-path and melded into the ocean of man and beast.

"What is this?" An angry lacerta voice hissed, just before there was the flash of a blade, resulting in a violent clash of metal upon metal.

I quickly wove my way through the living sea of soldiers in order to reach a potentially deadly and very much unneeded situation...

"Prohibere!" Meeka conjured...

(Silence!)

The lacerta warrior was statuesque, still very much alive, angry and confused, as was a loyal orc soldier, who had joined the Royal Army to gain respect for his people... also alive and aware.

"This," Meeka said to the lacerta warrior, (who had his sword raised above his own head in a striking pose,) as she motioned to the orc, (who had **his** sword out in a defensive pose,) "is a friend... FRIEND." The wizard then looked up and visually located Bolla, "Does he understand what I am telling him?"

"Yes," Bolla answered, "he understands quite well, all of my warriors and archers understand and speak the common language of man."

Thinking ahead, I asked one of the Royal Soldiers to loan me his shield, and then, holding it securely between the lacerta's sword and the orc's head, I had Meeka reverse her spell... I braced for the impact.

"Procedere," the wizard conjured.

The lacerta's sword came down and stopped, mere centimeters away from striking the shield, which I had on my arm; the orc continued to duck away.

A relieved laugh softly spread throughout the ranks and then gradually became loud conversation once more.

The orc and lacerta soldiers grasped wrists and claimed friendship, as my companions and I melded back into the sea of weapons, armor and flesh.

"Thanks, Meeka," I said to the wizard, "that was quick thinking!"

Meeka just laughed and proceeded to say, "No, I purposely tried to stay near the orcs when the two 'waves' joined together because I figured a clash of **some kind** would happen, especially whenever orcs are involved. Oddly enough, it was a lacerta that started it. I stand corrected."

I laughed as well, saying, "Our orcs were forewarned of the possibility of the lacerta being present and not to engage them."

"Well," she countered, "orcs aren't always the 'strongest spell in the book.'"

I laughed again and gave her a smile, and then sought out Brother Fost.

I am appointing you, Brother Fost, to be our Official Lead Healer and master mapper." I announced, as Sir Quinn, Commander Vlad and Bolla began to mix and divide the combined army into smaller units.

"Agreed!" Brother Fost joyfully announced, "Do I get an armed party to stand guard for me as I make the master map?"

"Pick your team." I smiled and said as I swept my hand across the sea of soldiers.

"Well, I would like to choose our original team, but that would compromise the structural integrity of the army as a whole, so, why don't you pick out a team for me?" The halfling priest requested.

I called over Loher and Meeka, "Loher, I need you to pick out your two best archers and Meeka, I could really use the best mage you've got."

Both women smiled, nodded their heads at Brother Fost and then vanished back into the crowd.

Moments later, two female elves wielding longbows arrived and a young, very young, human boy followed close behind; I eyed the boy, questioningly.

The boy flashed a toothy grin back at me.

"Well!" Brother Fost exclaimed when he saw the boy, "I had almost forgotten about you! Onh only knows why though."

The boy grinned back.

"You **know** this child?" I asked the priest, quite surprised.

"Indeed!" The priest cried in delight, "This is Kuchoff; we met below deck on The Scorpion on the way here. He is **very** powerful!"

"Well, okay," I chuckled, "if you're satisfied with him, he's all yours." I turned around and was about to walk away until...

"Meeka wouldn't have chosen him as her best if he was anything less than what you had asked for," a hauntingly familiar voice spat from behind.

I quickly spun back around, just to gaze eye to eye with... myself. (Myself?)

Realizing that this was a 'mirror image' spell, obviously casted by the boy, I (we) smiled and the mirror image of myself and I (we) agreed with the decision at the very same time. (Entertaining, but uncomfortable none the less.)

"He **is** her best," the other McLaaud said, as he slowly vanished into thin air, my voice trailing off after him. (Odd.)

(My heart skipped a beat.)

Kuchoff just stood there, smiling his goofy toothy grin at me, "Six," he said, "almost seven."

"How old are you, Boy?" I asked, and then suddenly realized that he had answered **before** I had asked the question.

I shook my head as if trying to clear out some cobwebs, astounded and impressed with the child's abilities.

"That's enough, Kuchoff," Brother Fost chortled and affectionately put his hand on the boy's head to draw him closer.

Unless you're an identical twin, it's not every day that you encounter your own doppelganger, magical or otherwise.

I slowly, thoughtfully mingled into the crowd to find some extra soldiers for the master mapping team, "Commander Vlad!" I called out, gaining his attention, "I need you to spare a few of your defenders for our master mapping team."

"As you wish," Commander Vlad agreed, regally clicked his heels, spun around and disappeared back into the crowd.

I returned back to Brother Fost and his team.

As I arrived, I found a table, a gathering of some rather comfortable looking chairs around it, a large spread of clean parchment, a pile of charcoal sticks upon the table and Brother Fost, Kuchoff and a dozen or so rabbits below it.

(Not again!)

I cleared my throat...

(Poof!)

The rabbits vanished.

(Thank the Gods!)

Brother Fost and a still grinning Kuchoff crawled out from beneath the table.

"A very nice set-up you have here," I said, gesturing toward the table, chairs and supplies.

"Kuchoff is quite efficient," the priest conceded with a smile and patted the boy on the head. "Wouldn't you agree?"

"Indeed," I agreed, quite impressed with the child's magical skills.

Kuchoff was **still** grinning.

Just then, five very large and very armed soldiers marched up to the table and stopped, their leader spoke up, "Sir, Commander Vlad ordered us to report to the master mapping team for duty."

All five soldiers clicked their heels and stood erect in formal attention.

"There's your team, Brother Fost, you're in charge," I said as I turned with a smile and a wave of my hand, blending back amongst the soldiers in the crowd.

•◆•

"McLaaud!" I heard Loher call from my right.

I turned to look for her.

"McLaaud," she said as she caught up to me and began to lead me toward a group, "I have our team assembled over here, ready to go and awaiting your command."

We arrived at a small mixed team of men and elves… and one dwarf, Balt.

"**Our** team?" I asked, "Why don't you and Balt have your own teams?"

I then looked and noticed that the base camp/command post was quickly emptying out as the many, many teams were going this way and that way, spreading out to make sure that every millimeter of the new cave was covered and mapped.

"Ye need a team," Balt stated.

"We volunteered," Loher added.

"So," I asked, "who's in charge?"

"Na meself, Mate," Balt spat, "I be no leader."

Loher let one of her enchanting and very rare smiles slip, "**You're** the ranger, I'll cover **your** back," she said as she twanged her bowstring and winked.

The awful sounds of battle abruptly rang out, turning our jovial mood into one of utter concern.

Instinctively taking the command that was so eagerly given to me, "**Let's move, team!**" I boomed as we all took off running toward the sounds of the ongoing scrimmage.

We rounded a corner and encountered an uncountable number of olyame violently attacking a mapping team.

Humanoid corpses already began littering the ground, the blood flowed in streams.

(Unlike vampires, the olyame do not drink their victim's blood, they let it drain.)

"Illuminare!" Our mage, a mage from within, Loher and I all coincidentally conjured together.

(Loher and I had taken courses from Meeka while still aboard The Scorpion.)

Several blasts of 'light' spells suddenly illuminated the cavern, overlapping each other, temporarily stunning the winged nightmares.

Arrows sang as they charged through the air, as I too, quickly struggled to string my own bow.

Loher let an arrow rip through the air at one of the flying beasts, which made contact, sending the creature to the now, body-covered floor.

Like a madman, Balt burst into the cavern, flung his Great Axe through the air and sliced one olyame cleanly in half; the Great Axe continued through the air and cleaved the wing of another, sending it too, to the ground, flopping and flailing about.

The injured olyame was set upon by blade-wielding ground forces and was quickly chopped into pieces.

Screams of fear, confusion, frustration, anger and pain echoed throughout the cavern and drowned out the constant sound of the raging, rushing river, the water had begun to flow red with the blood that had drained from the olyame's victims.

(...they let it drain...)

More teams rushed in to join in the (slaughter) fight, as another volley of arrows, including those from the bows of Loher and mine, darkened the air like a swarm of angry bees.

(Xobish!)

A half dozen or more olyame literally crashed and burned to the ground, as our arrows and another blast of 'light' spells met their targets with deadly precision.

The ground was littered – piled – with hundreds of bodies, humanoid and olyame, the metallic odor of blood, mixed with the putrid stench of acrid smoke from the burning flesh.

The combination overpowered the senses and stung the eyes of us all; all I could see, smell and taste was...

DEATH!

The echoing screams finally stopped except for the residual echoes of screams within my head.

I saw a mage or two scurrying about, extinguishing the flames from the still smoldering bodies.

The air began to clear as the teams began to slowly return to the base camp to regroup and reassemble.

Brother Fost and a few other Clerics began to heal the wounded, while a group of dwarves began to repair damaged weapons and armor.

Wizards and other magic-using members gathered in a circle to combine strength and summon up the spells necessary for the survival of the remaining army.

This was needed if we were to encounter another wave of the dreaded olyame.

✦

After a final head count, it was determined that the losses from one-hundred fifteen or so soldiers, archers and mages of the combined army were:

Sixteen Lacerta

Four Orcs

Four Men

Three Elves

One Dwarf

A total of twenty-eight were lost.

An estimated three-hundred Olyame were destroyed.

(Also one Troll, which started the original fire, as that is the only way to completely destroy a Troll without it regenerating severed limbs and multiplying.)

Score Board: Army: 300+ - Olyame: 28

Acceptable losses for such a strong victory.

I was quite surprised to see that several of the soldiers, over half, had taken a meal after the battle.

I was feeling sick to my own stomach, so the thought of food only made me sicker, but to each his own.

After only a few hours, the Royal Army was rearing and ready to go, despite our losses; they had a taste of blood (some for the first time) and wanted more.

Morale was also surprisingly high, as songs of praise for our young King were invented and sung; the songs were quickly adopted by most and rang out throughout the caverns.

It was definitely a time to behold.

The maps that were sketched out were all turned in to Brother Fost in exchange for pieces of clean parchment, on which to sketch even more of the tunnels and paths that were yet unexplored.

The teams had actually discovered parts of the caves that even the lacerta had no prior knowledge of; the master map was forming quite nicely.

According to the lacerta, the only areas that they knew of that remained to be mapped were a few rooms that are supposed to be empty, and then the pirate's treasure chamber, unless more was discovered in the meantime, like before.

We decided that we would split up into two teams, one for each room that was left.

After a room was searched and mapped, a lacerta within each group would lead the team to the entrance of the treasure chamber and wait for the second team to arrive.

We would all regroup as a whole to explore and map out the treasure chamber, as it would be far safer that way in case of pirate interference.

My team, led by Sir Quinn, consisted of five of the original six of us, (Brother Fost stayed behind to continue the master map,) as well as an equal portion of the army to make up the difference.

As we marched on to our unexplored room, I was made aware that young Kuchoff was walking by my side as he reached up and took hold of my free hand; he looked up and gave me that same goofy, toothy grin.

I was becoming quite fond of that grin, and the boy had a strange, sort of knowing glint in his eyes, as if he knew some sort of an important secret that he chose to keep all to himself.

He sure was powerful; I can honestly tell you that.

We entered our pre-assigned room, and the mappers carefully began to sketch out the area.

Loher walked and searched the perimeter of the room, periodically stopping to look closely at the floor or wall.

On one of her many stops, she scanned the wall and then squeezed her hand into a crevice.

While turning her hand within the crevice, she pushed on an apparently hidden pressure plate with her other hand, or one of her feet, only she knew.

There was a soft, interior click and the wall began to shift, quite like the secret passage into the Ferrum Mons.

"McLaaud, Quinn, I found a secret door," Loher sang out as the door slid open.

"Ain't a secret no more, Lass," Balt mused.

The mappers quickly and carefully mapped it all out.

The secret door opened into a wide, dark passage that led almost parallel with the passage to the pirate's treasure chamber.

"Illuminare!" Meeka conjured and the passage lit up nicely.

Kuchoff smiled up at her and she affectionately smiled back.

Cautiously, we entered through the secret door and slowly began to follow it, searching and mapping as we went.

Kuchoff swiftly let go of my hand and scampered off ahead of me, "I'll protect you," he said, looking back over his shoulder.

Loher glanced at me smiling and shot me a look as if to say, 'Awww.'

I smiled and rolled my eyes, but not so the kid could see me do it.

Soon, the air became dank, warm and moist; my skin began to crawl with an uneasy, foreboding feeling, almost as if we were knowingly trespassing through a daemon forest.

I looked around from face to face and could plainly see that I was not the only one affected by this feeling.

The passage abruptly ended at another wall and using the same technique, Loher located and opened yet another secret door.

This door led to an open, dimly lit room.

As soon as the door opened, warm, dank air blasted us like... I guess like the hot breath from a very large dog, and it smelled that way too.

We stayed for a moment, just outside of that room so the mappers could sketch out what they could see and so Loher could scan the entrance for secrets and traps.

There were none, but by the time we were ready to proceed inward, the whole team, including Commander Vlad and his half, had caught up to us and were waiting in the corridor behind us.

Commander Vlad had made his own way up to the front, and said to me in a low voice so that no one else could hear him, "I have a bad feeling about this."

I gave him a nod of understanding.

"What do you think is up ahead?" Loher asked.

Sir Quinn cut in from behind me, "Press on ahead, let's find out!" He said impatiently.

"Go on ahead, Knight," Loher spat, annoyed with the knight's false bravery and overwhelming sense of duty.

Wordlessly, the knight took the lead with a physical arrogance that was unbecoming, even for a knight.

"'E's gonna git 'imself kilt," Balt avowed, "er' worse."

Loher and I nodded our agreements and then pressed on to follow the rather foolhardy and rambunctious knight.

As we continued, Loher scanned each and every inch of the walls, floor and ceiling, as the mappers continued to sketch away our progress.

Besides the two secret doors that led us thus far, Loher had found nothing new.

We turned a corner into a sort of hallway that led straight down about fifty paces and then turned left.

After we turned left, the hallway widened out into an odd shaped small room where we finally caught up to Sir Quinn and a few other eager beavers.

A huge door took up most of the far wall of this room.

"It's locked," Sir Quinn moaned.

Loher calmly scanned the small room to find nothing of true interest and then she finally went to the door.

After a few seconds of rummaging around through her personal effects, she produced two small tools.

Quickly, quietly and quite efficiently, the thief picked the lock to the door in just under five seconds.

Sir Quinn was well impressed, and he made a move to push open the door, but the elven maiden roughly shoved him out of the way.

"What are you trying to do?" Loher hissed, "Get us **all** killed?"

The knight looked up at her from down on the floor with a hurt and very angry look written across his face, "What do you mean?" He barked.

By this time, the whole team had assembled around the pair.

"Listen to this door!" She snapped, but the knight just looked confused, "Put your ear to this door and **listen!**" She ordered.

Reluctantly, the knight rose to his feet, walked to the door and pressed his ear up against it.

After a few seconds, he wrinkled his nose and shook his head, "I hear nothing."

The rogue scowled and showed her teeth and then viciously pointed at the door, "Keep listening, you **fool!**"

The knight pressed his ear harder to the door and stuck his index finger into his other ear to block out the unwanted sounds around him...

He closed his eyes to help himself concentrate...

A few seconds later, his eyes sprung open – Wide...

Mixed messages of confusion and horror were swimming upon his features...

"What **is** that?" He whispered.

Chapter Nine

TRICKERY

Slowly and quietly, Loher opened the door.

It swung open wide enough to show a very large, fairly well-lit chamber that easily housed mounds upon mounds of gold, silver and copper coins, golden statues, trinkets, chalices, along with other valuable objects including enchanted weapons and armor and various precious jewels of all shapes, sizes and colors.

Mixed among all of that treasure, we saw the bones of many dead humanoid bodies, and we wondered how they had gotten there if this place was such a secret.

Everything was covered by a thick coating of spider webs and dust, showing us approximately just how long it had been since anything had been disturbed in this area.

The dank dog breath stench seemed to flow from this room, thick enough to taste and almost thick enough to actually see.

The smell was overpowering as many of the soldiers had doubled over and became violently ill, all the while, we could no longer hear the rushing of the river, but instead, a heavy pulsating rumble-like sound made the very **air** dance around us adding to the discomfort.

"Look!" A human soldier suddenly bellowed, "The pirate's treasure!"

Before anyone had the chance to stop him, he blindly rushed straight into the room, only to be floored seconds later by a dozen or so poisonous darts that were set as a trap and triggered as soon as he stepped on a pressure plate in the floor.

"The Fool!" Loher hissed.

"Poor Monty," Balt commented as he lowered and shook his head, "more bones ta add ta th' collection."

"We must be near another entrance to this cave," Loher stated.

"Why do you say that?" A soldier asked.

"Look at all of these humanoid bones," she said as she swept her hand across the room. "If we are the first to have entered this cave, where did all of these bones come from? There has to be an old entrance near here."

The soldier nodded in understanding and agreement and then stepped away from the door.

Sir Quinn had also backed away from the door and silently vowed to be more careful in the future. "Th- that c-could have been m-m-me," the knight stuttered.

Kuchoff shot Sir Quinn that same toothy grin and knowing gaze, blinked a few times and then quickly scampered away.

Loher inspected the doorway for more triggers and traps, but only found those that were already spent by the late Monty.

She cautiously entered the treasure-filled room on her hands and knees, searching as she moved; looking for pressure plates, buttons, trip wires, levers or anything else that could be a trigger for a trap.

When she finally reached Monty's corpse, she checked for signs of life, just to make sure, but found none.

The elven maiden looked back at us and drew her finger across her throat, indicating to the rest of us that Monty was indeed dead.

She then continued her search for triggers and traps, passing the body, leaving it temporarily behind.

All of a sudden, she stopped.

Once again, she rummaged through her belongings and brought out an odd shaped tool.

She dug the tool into the floor between two flat stones that had been used to tile the floor, and then flattened her body against the floor next to the tool.

Pressing down on the tool, she triggered an extremely large spiked hammer that swung down from the ceiling, as if meant to impale the elf.

The weaponized trap had missed her flattened body, but not by much.

Carefully, she searched more of the area; still keeping low to the ground and after several more minutes of searching, it seemed that she was satisfied that there were no more traps.

Motioning for the rest of us to enter, the elven maiden rose to her feet.

Although we had Loher's 'okay' to safely enter the room, we were still extremely cautious on the way in.

The mounds of treasure sparkled and dazzled in beautiful radiance from the light that seemed to come from everywhere, yet, nowhere.

"No one touches a thing!" Commander Vlad ordered, and everyone, including my team, whole heartedly agreed, still wary of traps that may still be hidden amongst the treasure.

"I thinked ye was **dead**, Mate!" Balt exclaimed, as we all witnessed Monty slowly rise to his feet and stagger toward us.

Then, we noticed that the other bones that were strewn about, among the piles of treasure, began to connect together and form into full skeletons that slowly reached for weapons that were conveniently placed where each new body was formed.

"Undead!" Commander Vlad warned, "Soldiers, spread out and stand ready! Mappers, continue mapping, but make haste! Archers!"

The soldiers clicked their heels and obediently spread out as ordered; some covered the mappers who quickly logged everything their eyes could see.

Skeleton warriors seemed to appear literally from everywhere and the pulsing air seemed to grow stronger, perhaps even faster.

"Is there a cleric among us?" I called out, "A priest?" I asked, "Do we have a priest? Where's Brother Fost?"

"Brother Fost stayed back at the command post," a voice called out from somewhere among the rattling bones.

Loher unexpectedly gripped my elbow and flashed me one of those beautiful smiles, "It's alright," she whispered close in my ear, and then notched an arrow onto her bowstring.

I drew my sword and we both stood together, ready to defend.

(The pulsing air seemed to grow stronger still...)

"Wait for them to attack us first," the commander announced, "they may not strike unless the treasure is disturbed! We **must** follow the Royal Rules of Engagement!"

The Royal Soldiers all clicked their heels and grunted out an affirmation.

At first, the commander's words seemed as if they may ring true until Monty the zombie wildly, but ineffectively, swung a closed fist in Balt's direction.

"Awe, come now, Laddy," Balt quipped, "ye dinna even make contact wit me. Try again!"

A faint murmur of laughter rose up among the ranks.

Monty the zombie then clumsily yanked his sword from its sheath.

"Now ye be talkin', Boy-o!" The dwarven fighter mused, "Oi! Commander, is **tis** count'n as a attack?"

Commander Vlad studied the zombie's movements as it mindlessly raised its sword and futilely swung it at Balt's unflinching head.

(A swing and a miss… strike two!)

"Well," the commander began, "if you really **can't** wait for your opponent to make actual **contact—**"

Monty swung and missed again…

(Strike three – yer **Out!**)

Balt half smiled as he raised his Great Axe over Monty's head…

…Then, "I be real sorry 'bout tis Mate," he said, as he just let gravity take the weight of the Great Axe down to see just how sharp the blade actually was.

Gravity truly enjoyed doing its job, as it invisibly grasped a hold on the Great Axe and effortlessly drove the blade cleanly through Monty's head, all the way to the bridge of his nose, where it stopped and asked for a little push.

"**That** is one **heavy** axe!" Sir Quinn mused, raising a chuckle from within the ranks.

"Sharp as well, Knight," Balt added, which brought forth even more chuckles.

Balt pulled his axe free from the cleaved head of the now still zombie.

(Royal Army: 1 – Undead Army: 0)

A Royal Soldier suddenly went down with an agonizing groan; I witnessed one of the skeleton warriors yank its bloody sword from the dying soldier's chest, as the rest of the skeletal warriors unexpectedly jumped into action, as if some sort of silent signal had been made.

"**NOW!**" The commander ordered, as he bashed in the skull of the closest skeleton with the blunt ended handle of his sword, and then swung around and lopped off the skull of a second skeleton with a single stroke from the same blade.

Three more of the Royal Soldiers were grudgingly taken by surprise, as a half dozen of the grisly undead unexpectedly jumped out from a large pile of coins; the three poor souls never even stood a chance as they were quickly overpowered and grievously submitted.

Loher let an arrow fly that found purchase in the breast bone of a skeletal foe that was about to bury its axe into the back of an unsuspecting young Royal Soldier; the force of the impact of the spinning arrow shattered the bone and crumbled the rest of the walking horror to dust.

The three fallen Royal Soldiers gradually rose to their feet and took up arms against their former comrades, which in turn, hesitated to return the attack upon the familiar faces of **their** former friends.

This was an unfortunate setback for us, as the three new zombies gruesomely cut down all but a few of **my** team's remaining allied soldiers, turning **them** into potential zombies as well.

The nightmare was only getting worse.

I took a running start at a group of three skeletons, I came in low and tried to hook my sword into all three sets of ribcages; I succeeded in hooking two of the three, as the last one dodged away toward the closest wall.

I swung the two that I had hooked into the third, consecutively smashing all three against the wall; they exploded into a burst of bone-shards and dust.

One of the last remaining Royal Soldiers abruptly called out my name, making me spin around, just in time to see him sacrifice himself to save me, by diving in front of a large skeletal (dog?) animal of some sort; that brave, selfless soldier saved me from what might have been a substantial amount of pain – at best – perhaps even death.

The soldier screamed out briefly as the bony beast fatally gored him just below the chest and tore out his guts.

Angrily, I smashed the 'dog' into pieces before it could fully complete its gory feat and then I mercifully sliced off the fallen soldier's head and kicked it far away so he could not unwillingly rise up against me.

The room was rapidly filled with what sounded like whip-cracks; I quickly turned to see Kuchoff and Meeka launching 'ice balls' at the advancing undead army.

Shards of bone and ice began to rain down on us as the pair of mages exterminated wave after wave of the undead army, as it ceaselessly marched on toward us.

Loher and her archers joined in as the blade-wielding 'ground-pounders' took a short and well deserved rest behind the line.

After a while, the sound of the frigid volley of 'ice balls', arrows and bone cracks began to thin and drown out as the familiar sound of marching feet began to overpower our very thoughts within our minds.

The intense marching sounded as if it was coming from behind the wooden doorway from which we had arrived.

Not only were the undead advancing in waves from within the mounds of treasure, but now a **second** army was advancing from behind!

"I think we're in trouble!" Sir Quinn urgently called out to the team, as yet another small group of Royal Soldiers went down in a gout of spraying blood and dismembered limbs.

"Regroup!" Commander Vlad ordered.

Slowly, what was left of the Royal Army began to regroup in a centralized location, standing back-to-back in a tight revolving circle.

My team and I joined in to strengthen the group.

Loher, joined by the rest of the archers, stood in the center of the circle, so when a strategically placed dwarf came around in the circle, there would be enough room to fire off an arrow or two at the enemy.

Waves of the undead continued to ebb in as the unknown army closed in on us.

The sound of marching feet finally slowed to a stop, and for a split second, all went quiet, except for a few nervous gulps of fear and the rattling of the advancing bones.

A large volley of arrows swiftly swarmed in like angry wasps, pinning down the advancing undead threat.

Two by two, lacerta warriors stormed into the chamber, engaging the undead.

Zombies and skeletons fell at an even faster rate as our mixed army joined forces once again.

"We decided to come find you when you didn't show up." Bolla called over the sound of the raging battle, "That's when we found the hidden passage propped open with a rock. Nice thinking!"

"You didn't happen to bring Brother Fost along, did you?" I asked, trying not to sound anxious.

Bolla yelled something in the lacerta tongue to one of the other lacerta warriors that was standing nearest to the door, who, in turn, yelled the same thing back out through the door to someone else.

A moment later, the halfling priest was escorted into the room by two heavily shielded lacerta warriors.

The wide-eyed priest took one look around at the dire scene, smiled and then quickly climbed to the top of a mound of coins.

He closed his eyes and raised both of his hands high above his head and then calmly said, "Ad Mortem."

Instantly, as if someone had pulled a lever, the undead army ceased all movement and fell at our feet like marionette puppets that suddenly had their strings cut all at once.

A low cheer gradually erupted from among the surviving ranks.

Brother Fost smiled – but his smile rapidly turned to a death mask of blood-curdling horror; terrified out of his wits, his face turned ashen white, and it looked as though he was about to faint.

"D-d-dr-dra-g-g-o-n-..." the priest stammered, as he slid down to the floor from high atop the treasure pile.

"What did you say?" Meeka asked as she quickly knelt down beside him.

"It **sounded** like he said, 'Dragon,'" a soldier laughed nervously, as he slowly looked all around himself.

Brother Fost swallowed hard, vigorously nodded his head in affirmation and pointed a finger in a direction that was blocked by many large piles of coins.

"You saw... a **dragon?**" I asked, as I gently put my hand on his shoulder.

The halfling nodded a 'yes'.

"Over there?" I asked, pointing in the same direction that he did.

Again, he nodded a 'yes' and I began to become a bit nervous myself.

The rest of our companions began to edge closer in.

"Umm, Brother Fost?" I asked.

The priest looked me directly in the eyes.

"What **color** was the dragon?" I asked calmly.

The halfling gave me a half-crazy smile and opened his hand, a large emerald dropped onto my boot and then rolled across the floor… "Green," he whispered.

Meeka got a peculiar look in her eyes and then a rabid smile adorned her lips.

She pulled her fiery red hair back into a tight 'pony tail,' and then fished her magic tome from deep within her cloak.

She then leaned down and gently kissed Brother Fost on his forehead whispering, "Don't worry, Wee One, just give me a few moments, okay?"

Kuchoff pulled **his** tome out from what seemed like thin air, and ran to join her.

They smiled toothy grins at each other and began to compare notes.

I turned to Bolla, "I thought you said there **was no** dragon!" I spat, and deliberately poked my index finger into his scaly chest with each word to show emphasis.

The lacerta holy man backed up and raised his…(hands?) in a defensive posture.

A few lacerta warriors raised their weapons and looked as if they were about to attack me, but Balt and Sir Quinn stepped in the way with weapons drawn, shaking their heads.

The lacerta decided to back down.

"I **swear**," Bolla hissed, "we honestly knew nothing of this dragon, or this treasure. This isn't even the **pirates'** treasure room!"

I stopped poking and backed off, "**Not**, the pirates' treasure?" I echoed.

Bolla shook his head, "No, the pirates' treasure is down in the cove, by the water, in **chests**… mostly."

I felt a tap on my shoulder…

"Are we actually going to **attack** this dragon?" Commander Vlad interrupted.

I turned my attention to the old man, "No," I laughed, "that would go against your Royal Rules of Engagement, now, wouldn't it?" I smiled. "We are going to **attempt** to go peacefully **speak** to the dragon and tell it that all we want to do is simply map out the area and **leave**."

"Then... what are your wizards doing?" The commander asked, and pointed his thumb at the magical pair, hovering over their books.

"We like to call it...'insurance.'"

Anxious for action, the blade-wielding portion of the mixed Royal Army held cover behind great mounds of treasure, as Loher carefully searched the room around the sleeping dragon for traps.

A team of highly skilled archers, both lacerta and elf (myself included,) stood spread out, with our bows ready.

The two wizards, Meeka and Kuchoff, began to quietly chant their ancient spells.

After what seemed like an eternity, Loher gave the 'all clear' signal and a mapping team made up of only elves, quickly and quietly, made their way around the room, mapping everything they could see – including the sleeping dragon.

As the mapping team worked their way across the room, a smaller attachment of archers and I moved along with them; we noticed that the strange pulsing throb we all had been experiencing was actually the rhythmic breathing of the sleeping beast, as was (now quite obvious to us,) that hot, dank, dog-breath stench.

From a distance, the sleeping dragon looked solid green with a (possible) white belly and chest, but up close, the closest I have ever been to a dragon either live or dead, its huge iridescent green scales looked as if they were formed out of emerald chips, and the white underbelly was actually a bluish-grey color, quite like that of a pearl.

The beast itself was approximately fifteen or twenty large paces long, **not** including the tail, which was wrapped tightly around its body.

It was difficult to determine how wide the body of the beast was, because we could not get around it to measure.

There was just too much treasure piled up on the far side to get an accurate measurement, but if I had to guess, I would have to say it was approximately five to seven large paces wide, a great beast, and this was only a youngster!

(We could tell by the bright shine on its nice, straight, protruding teeth.)

The mapping team had completed their task and Loher had found an exit passage out of the room.

The sound of a (class two) rushing river could be heard from beyond this way.

Once again, Loher gave the signal that all was clear, so I motioned to the rest of the (blade-wielding) army to follow, with a wave of my hand.

Loher had taken up her bow and joined me, along with the other archers and the pair of (now silent) wizards, as we all stood ready.

The blade-wielding soldiers moved not-so-silently through, followed by the—

"Its eye just opened!" Loher gasped, loud enough for me to hear.

"It's awake!" Someone else cried and I heard several bowstrings draw back.

"Hold your fire!" I called out and heard my order repeated a few times down the line of archers; "Meeka?" I called.

"Ignis, argumentum, scutum," the wizard ventriloquised at me.

An unseen force unexpectedly pushed me back a half of a step and I found myself standing directly in front of the dragon's slowly rising head and tiredly focusing eyes.

My heart felt as if it was about to burst right out through my ribcage and my knees wanted to go limp, but I locked them straight and I suddenly felt like I had to pee.

Time seemed to slow down for me as I watched the dragon's head rise up from what **was** eye level to me, to a full ten feet or more above my own head.

Drool oozed out from the corners of its dagger-like tooth infested mouth, as it (slowly) licked its lips.

The putrid, nefarious stench of rotten flesh that was probably stuck between a few of its enormous teeth assaulted my senses and almost made me gag.

The dragon, now fully awake, looked right down at me, if not **through** me, blinked a few times, drew back a quick, sharp breath and then spat out a huge ball of bright red and orange flame that completely engulfed me for what seemed like a full minute.

Two things happened within that minute: One – Meeka's 'fire proof shield' spell worked, I felt no heat at all and there was absolutely no damage to my body, armor or surrounding area within said spell; and Two – I no longer had to pee.

The young dragon looked at me with utter confusion plastered upon its face; I could hear Meeka quietly chanting a new spell from behind a large pile of gems, and **that's** when I suddenly noticed that I was standing out there completely alone.

However, from the corner of my eye, I could just barely see hidden archers with their loaded bows aimed and ready.

(I felt a bit better after seeing that.)

The dragon tried to cook me again, this time with a longer, larger blast.

Again, Meeka's spell (thankfully) held up, confusing the young dragon even more.

I held up my hands, "I desire no quarrel with you, Dragon," I said as calmly as I could make my voice sound.

"Kusagi," the dragon spoke.

"Bless you!" I offered, as if the dragon had sneezed.

"My name," it said, "is Kusagi."

I nodded my head in understanding, "McLaaud," I offered, "Thunor McLaaud of Larix." I bowed low, but still kept my eyes directly on him.

"Ahh," Kusagi sighed, "the Seolfer Wudu... this is **my** grotto, Elf," he said, glancing from one side to the other. "What are you doing in **my grotto!?!**" He roared.

"Simply mapping the area, I was about to leave," I admitted, composing myself.

"Where is the map?" He asked, eyeing me closely.

Thinking quickly, I acted like I was checking through my gear and when I came up empty, I stated, "You must have burned it up with your breath."

"**Good!**" He said with a grin, "I don't want any maps of my grotto floating around for others to see."

"Yep!" I feigned a chuckle, "It's gone," I said, showing my empty hands. "I guess I'll just forget the whole thing... and, be on my way!" I said, as I slowly began to edge my way closer to the door, forcing another fake laugh.

"Where do you think **you're** going?" Kusagi asked as he rose half way to his feet.

(I stopped laughing.)

"Well," I said, trying to sound confident, "you obviously don't want to be disturbed any longer, so I figured—"

The dragon roared out a sound that shook my very soul, as well as the whole grotto.

The roar leveled a few piles of treasure and exposed my companions that were still masked within.

"Intruders?" Shocked and deeply upset, he let out another loud roar that was more intimidating and vicious than the first.

"Ignis, argumentum, scutum, omnes!!" Both wizards commanded in unison, just in time, before Kusagi breathed a very large, but very weak cloud of fire across the treasure piles in an attempt to cook the mixed army; some of the thinner coins and smaller golden baubles had melted, but the cloud was not strong enough to melt a whole lot.

(The wizards' spells worked well, once again!)

"Quickly!" I cried to the team, "Get behind some gold! He doesn't want to melt his gold!"

"Aim and **fire!**" Loher ordered the archers in a loud and commanding voice; a volley of a few dozen arrows soared over the treasure mounds and toward the dragon.

Kusagi just laughed as he simply shrugged off the arrow volley as if it was a harmless swarm of flies, strategically spitting concentrated, almost gooey (Napalm) fireballs at us.

Two unlucky victims ran screaming, abhorrently aflame, from their cover, trying futilely to extinguish themselves.

"We're going to have to face him head-on!" Commander Vlad grimly announced to those that were close enough to him to hear.

"I nominate meself," Balt bravely announced with a wicked smile.

"Aye an' me. I be wit ye, Brudder," another dwarven fighter volunteered.

"Donna' forgets meself as well," a third dwarf announced, making me realize that these were the same two dwarves that accompanied Balt on the ferry and in the 'Broken Blade' later on that night.

The dwarven trio was beginning to rise, preparing for the attack, when Kuchoff stopped them, "**Wait!**" The boy cried, "Join hands!"

The dwarves complied.

Kuchoff grasped the two available hands, completing a circle of four.

"Ignis, argumentum, scutum, omnes!!" The young wizard incanted and then let their hands free.

"Me thanks be to ye, Boy-o," Balt smiled and rubbed the boy's head.

(Screams and hisses of pain erupted as a half dozen or more unfortunate lacerta warriors were caught in a huge flaming wave.)

The dwarven wrecking crew shouted an eerie war cry as they scrambled over the towering mounds of gold, silver and precious stones.

Kusagi quickly snorted out three very well aimed gobs of liquid fire at the advancing dwarves, but the fire just rolled off of them like water on a duck's back.

Balt's Great Axe, still dripping with Monty's grey brain matter, effortlessly cleaved off a few light grey scales, as it slammed into the dragon's lower chest; the removed scales toppled to the floor at Balt's feet.

He picked them up, "Use these as shields, Maties!" Balt called out, as he tossed a scale each to his brothers.

The second dwarf, wielding two swords, slipped the blade of one of his swords under another grayish scale and pried it up just enough to stab his other, longer, sword into soft pinkish flesh of the dragon's underbelly.

The dragon howled out in pain as the dwarf twisted the blade and then pulled it out at an angle, ducking away a moment later.

The third dwarf was not as lucky, as Kusagi's rear right foot came smashing down and crushed the stout warrior to a pulp.

(The result was like that of a grape underfoot.)

Kusagi raised his rear left foot and engaged his uncurling tail, but Balt anticipated this move and skillfully rolled out of the way in just enough time to elude the descending rear foot, but just a bit too late to successfully dodge the whipping tail.

He swiftly found himself colliding headlong into a stalagmite after a quick, short trip by air.

He shook his head, clearing out the daze and checked himself for damage, finding none; he smiled and roared out another war cry, returning to the fight.

(He solemnly vowed to grieve the loss of his fallen brother...later.)

"Tela!" Kuchoff summoned as he thrust his hand forward and then splayed his fingers, as if throwing an object toward the dragon.

As a matter of a fact, he **did** throw something, as five mid-sized missiles of concentrated energy erupted from around the boy's fingers in rapid succession and consecutively slammed into the beast, temporarily knocking it off balance.

A large gaping wound opened on the dragon's left side, exposing soft pink flesh, gushing large gouts of blood and gore.

The injured dragon let loose with another well aimed volley of flaming goo-balls that lobbed into the army.

Gelled flames poured onto and across the floor behind a slowly melting mound of gold; two dozen or so lacerta warriors were swallowed up into the molten mess of melted rock and precious metals.

"Kuchoff!" Meeka called, "Use your Psi energies on him!"

The child's face rapidly split into his famous toothy grin as he vigorously nodded his shaggy head, and then retreated behind a very large mound of coins.

"What is Kuchoff doing?" I asked, as I crouched under cover close to Meeka.

"Do you recall having a face-to-face conversation with Thunor McLaaud back at the base camp?" She reminded me.

"Meeka?" I asked, wondering if one of us had lost their mind, "**I'm** Thunor Mc... Ohh, I get it!" I smiled, as it finally dawned on me, "his 'mirror image' spell."

"That's not exactly what it is," Meeka explained, "Kuchoff uses a mind manipulation skill called 'Psionics.' Psionics enables the Psionisist to manipulate the mind of his subject and allow the subject to believe what the Psionisist **wants** the subject to believe. Get it?"

"I think I do," I admitted.

"Now, if you'll excuse me, I have to get ready for **my** part of the trick," she said as she scrambled over a small mound of gold, and lobbed an 'energy missile' at the dragon's head as her own cover fire.

"What??" I asked, slightly deafened from the throbbing explosion, but the wizard had already scurried away.

I saw a group of my companions huddled together behind a large treasure pile; I quickly crawled toward them.

"Oi, Mate," Balt chuckled, as I rolled into the shelter.

I nodded at the dwarf, a little out of breath, as Loher flashed me a smile and Brother Fost quickly checked me for wounds.

"Kuchoff and Meeka have a surprise in store for us all," I warned, "be ready!"

"What are they going to do?" Loher asked.

"It's na a se-prize, Lass, if 'e tells ye what it is," Balt teased.

Before anyone could laugh or have any reaction at all, a great and powerful roar erupted behind us from where we had to fight off the undead army; the grotto shook with fantastic rumblings.

Kusagi's attack pattern faltered and his eyes went wide and wild.

My heart began to beat frantically and all action gradually slowed or stopped, as the sound of very powerful footfalls and ultra-heavy breathing filled Kusagi's grotto.

Kusagi himself began to frantically look around and sniff the air as if he was suddenly aware of...

Meanwhile, Kuchoff, his arms held out like claws in front of him, stomping in great, exaggerated footsteps, stepped out from behind the large mound of coins that had hidden his slight retreat, his tiny frame was surrounded by the image of an extremely large iridescent dragon, whose scales reflected every known color.

(As well as many previously unknown colors.)

..."**Lord Avilyn!**" Kusagi gasped, "My King!"

We peered out in awe, unbelieving the sight we were beholding.

Young Kuchoff was successfully tricking the dragon, Kusagi, into believing that he was actually seeing the illustrious king of dragons, Lord Avilyn, **incarnate**.

"Bow to me, young Kusagi," Lord Avilyn (Kuchoff) majestically thundered.

Kusagi bowed in reverence, as low as a dragon could possibly get and groveled at the (Psionisist's) larger dragon's feet.

Loher nudged me and pointed behind the illusion at Meeka, whose hair was beginning to stand on end.

The young dragon continued to grovel as a very large energy bolt tore through the air, right through the image of Avilyn, from Meeka's hands, so it looked like it had come from the dragon king's mouth.

The bolt struck Kusagi full on the top of his head, sprawling him out on the floor, semi-conscious.

Kusagi slowly rose to his feet, quickly aimed and sneezed out a long flair that flowed harmlessly over Kuchoff's head, but went directly at Meeka, who had to dive and roll out of the way; but before she did, she fired off a double round of energy bolts that again, looked as if they were produced from Avilyn's maw and not the now hidden Meeka's hands.

The twin bolts crashed side-by-side into Kusagi's chest, knocking him back to the ground.

Sir Quinn took this chance and dove in for the kill, his sword shimmering with **death** dancing on its edge.

Loher launched a spinning arrow that met the soft, pink tissue of the dragon's left side, just as the knight's blade sunk in and twisted upward into the scale-less, exposed area of the dragon's chest.

The knight's blade was repeatedly stabbed in and out, slicing at least a half a dozen new wounds, as bright red blood gushed out like the rush of pressurized crude oil from a freshly struck well.

Kusagi roared out in pain once again and batted at the well-shielded knight, as he once again drew himself up to his unsteady feet; Sir Quinn calmly ducked and rolled, easily out of the swinging tail's way.

Meeka, hidden behind the wavering image of the dragon king, summoned another bolt of pure energy, aimed and let it go, driving it straight into the fresh wounds from Sir Quinn's blade; the power from the impact lifted the dragon completely off his feet and let gravity slam him violently to the ground, knocking the breath forcefully from his lungs.

A huge blasting, white-hot fountain of flame shot up like a molten pillar from the mouth of the beast and into the ceiling of the grotto, dislodging a stalactite which fell down, impaling the dragon like a wooden stake through a vampire's heart.

The image of the mighty Avilyn, now unneeded, began to fade as a victorious cheer burst forth from the now dwindling team.

The unnerving, pulsating throb of the dragon's breathing was finally gone and the low rushing sound of the nearby river ebbed in through the doorway.

After some discussion with Sir Quinn and Loher, we decided to leave the treasure where it was, for now, until we could return and properly locate and remove any and all existing traps that may be hidden within.

"My people and I will guard it with our lives. Hail, Lagu Ofer'Eal!" Bolla vowed with a click of his heels.

Of the original one-hundred fifteen able-bodied soldiers, the only survivors were:

Sir Quinn, Balt, Loher, Brother Fost, Meeka,

Kuchoff, Commander Vlad,

Bolla, Ollie, Drez,

Two Lacerta Warriors, Six Lacerta Archers,

Four Elven Archers,

Three Royal Soldiers,

And

Myself.

⸺◆⸺

"That was **amazing**!" Meeka exclaimed with a jovial laugh, as she hugged the pint-sized Psionisist.

How did you **do** that?" Another voice asked, as the praise continued and we exited the dead dragon's grotto.

The sound of the rushing river became louder the further we walked, leaving Bolla and his team in the grotto.

(The mappers continued to map out the way.)

Even after our grievous losses, our morale was still quite high and growing higher, as the air became thicker with moisture and began to smell faintly like the salty sea.

I think we are getting closer to the exit leading outside!" Sir Quinn announced excitedly, "I can smell the salt in the air!"

The whole team unconsciously slowed and began sniffing the air.

"I knew it," Loher said to herself and thought of the now dead young soldier, whom she had made this suggestion to before the undead battle.

Her thoughts were interrupted by the sounds of unfamiliar voices, but the echo was too great to make out language or words.

She silently got our attention and placed her finger over her lips to quiet us down.

"You hear something?" I whispered.

"I do," she quietly answered, "men, talking and laughing, I'm guessing they're the pirates that Bolla warned us about."

We slowly, quietly crept up on the men that were down by the water's edge and as we arrived within a short distance, but still out of sight, I motioned to the team to stay put.

"I'm going to stick to the shadows and get a bit closer to see who, or what they are," Loher said, as she quietly picked out two more elves and asked them to follow.

The three cloaked themselves and quite literally disappeared right before my very eyes and about fifteen minutes later, I felt a hand quickly slide over my mouth from behind, and it was probably a good thing as it turned out, the hand stifled a potentially loud gasp as I witnessed Loher step out of a rock wall, or so it seemed.

She let go of my face, "You'll **never** believe what we just saw!" She whispered with an odd gleam in her violet-purple eyes, she motioned us all back toward the grotto.

When we were a little less than half way back, Loher stopped. "There are pirates in the cove down there, unloading chests from their ship," she finally said.

"How many pirates?" I asked.

"How many crewmen were aboard The Scorpion?" She answered my question with a question.

I blinked my eyes a few times and shook my head as I realized exactly what she had meant, "You're right, I **don't** believe it."

"Wait a minute now, Lassie," Balt laughed, "Cap'n Waxx be a **pirate?**"

Loher nodded her head in affirmation.

"Waxx **knew** that we were going from one end of this cave to the other on a sweep and clear mission," Sir Quinn thought out loud, "we were **bound** to run into this area at **some** point. If he's actively conducting piracy here, while we are so obviously still in the area, he must not have intended to..."

⁘

"Keep it much of a secret, Mon," a voice from around the corner completed the knight's sentence.

Captain Waxx and two other pirates stepped out from around the corner. "I be won'drin when you'd be comin' round," Captain Waxx laughed.

"How did you know we were here?" Brother Fost asked, still a bit startled.

"Acshully, I was tinkin you'd steel be in de'ar wit de dragon," he said, "but den de roarin' stopped, so's we sneaked up 'ere ta do some peekin', Mon."

"So **you knew** there was a dragon up here?" I asked in full surprise.

"Dat be right, Mon," Waxx admitted with a chuckle, "but no worries, now dat de dragon be dead Mon, we can split up all de treasure. Call me share payment fer all de carrying of ya I done," he paused to think and then smiled wide, "An' all de carrying I'll be dooin' for ya in de ne'ar feu'cher, as well – Partner." He stuck out his hand as if to make a business deal.

Sir Quinn and I exchanged quick glances and then eyed the captain.

I turned to face my friends and asked, "What do you all think? We should take a vote."

The captain's hand was still poised, patiently waiting.

"Well," Sir Quinn began, "It **would** be nice to be able to get to where we needed to go, when we needed to get there. A ship would certainly help with that, but only if you can vow that there will be absolutely no piracy whilst we are on board."

Captain Waxx's face suddenly dropped for a moment, and it looked as though he was having difficulty in making a decision, but suddenly he began to smile, and agreed, "No worries, Mon. You be havin' me vow."

"Good," Brother Fost cheered, "my short legs get awfully tired with all of the walking we have done."

"Aye, meself agrees wit tat!" Balt quipped.

Meeka and Kuchoff stood silently with smiles on their faces and Commander Vlad simply shot his hands in the air and shook his head as if to say that he had nothing to contribute.

"Me men be more'n willin' an able to defend ya to de death if need be, so no worries, Mon," the captain added with his hand still patiently hanging in limbo.

"We still have to secure the treasure and check it thoroughly for traps before **any** of it gets moved," Loher warned.

"We was acshully plannin' to add **our** plunder to de dragon's booty, it'd be more s'cure dat wey anyhow," the captain promised, hand still waiting.

Sir Quinn remarked, "It will be up to our King to confirm the deal since the grotto and cove are part of the cave." The knight paused to gauge a reaction, there was none, then continued, "Assuming that he does, I can agree that the transportation alone will be well worth it."

I took one last look at my friends to gauge their reactions, but they were smiling and nodding.

I smiled and nodded as well and then grasped a hold on the ship captain's hand, we vigorously shook to our agreement on the deal we had just made.

"Welcome into our team, Captain Waxx," I said with much pleasure.

"Welcome aboard to yaselves," Captain Waxx returned. "We'll just have ta unload de plunder a might quicker if it's not all done by de time we return to de ship," he said as we all walked back down the tunnel toward the waiting Scorpion.

"Dey muss be all done," he said as we approached the ship.

There was no activity on land and minimal (if any) aboard the ship.

"Won't all of those chests have to be moved now Captain?" Brother Fost inquired as he pointed to the few hundred chests and piles of plunder, littering the cove.

"No worries," Waxx said with a smile as he pat the halfling priest on the back, "all in due time, boy, all in due time."

Chapter Ten

OPEN SEA

As we boarded The Scorpion, Captain Waxx began issuing orders and the crew, some eyeing us up and down, began to hustle about, performing their ordered tasks.

We exited the cave through the cove's entrance that was conveniently hidden by some tall strategically, yet naturally, placed rocks creating a sort of natural optical illusion.

The opening was difficult to see even now, knowing it was there.

We traveled through The Haze Cove, past the Yfel Holh Caves and after a few hours of zigging and zagging and making twists and turns, as the sun was about to set, we entered the Strait of Avilyn; we were making very good time, as we had a strong tailwind pushing us along as we headed southwest.

Evening came... as a joke to some, a few sailors asked us to be very quiet as the sun began to set, so we might be able to hear it sizzle as it submerged out of sight beneath the waves.

Brother Fost, Kuchoff and Meeka were a bit upset when they failed to hear the sound; the rest of us had to fight back our amused laughter.

The crew went ahead and sang songs and told tales of their once secret adventures as pirates; then my team shared what we could about the cave.

We dined on various species of sea creatures and steamed seaweed, which was actually quite tasty and according to the sailors, is also very healthy.

(Among other ailments, the seaweed cures and prevents scurvy, which is a common disease among sailors and pirates, resulting from a deficiency of vitamin C, characterized by weakness, anemia [when the blood is low in red blood cells] and spongy gums.)

After the meal, a large bottle of very potent rum was passed around until one by one, we either passed out drunk or fell asleep due to utter exhaustion.

In the morning, Loher woke me with word that we were being chased by a band of rival pirates.

Their ship was gaining on us slowly but surely.

I rose to my feet and peered over the side of The Scorpion at the advancing ship. "I could use some coffee," I said to myself, as I rubbed my aching, hung-over head.

The rival ship was quite a bit smaller than The Scorpion, therefore lighter, so the wind could push it at a quicker rate across the waves.

The Scorpion's captain and crew didn't seem very disturbed by the fact that we were being targeted by an enemy faction; in fact, **most** of them seemed to be quite pleased.

I wasn't sure if their calmness was just a ploy to keep us **all** calm, or if they were just so used to being attacked like this as if it was just a daily routine – but as of yet, we had not actually been attacked, we were only being chased – so far.

Loher appeared by my side and offered me a large mug of coffee.

I was so surprised and grateful, I couldn't help myself, I smiled and abruptly kissed the elven maiden, full on the mouth; she was quite surprised herself, but she never pulled away.

Feeling self-conscious, I lifted the mug and slowly drank the first half of the liquid before coming up for air.

Loher was still standing there, staring at me.

I shyly smiled and then drained the rest of the mug's contents; she was smiling as she took the empty mug and swiftly strode away.

"I think you may have put your pants on backwards," Sir Quinn quipped as he joined me on the deck.

"What is **that** supposed to mean?" I asked, laughing from embarrassment.

"That kiss," the knight laughed.

"You **saw** that?" I blushed.

The knight laughed again, "I have been seeing it coming for a while now, haven't **you?**" He asked with a smile and never took his gaze away from my face.

I sighed and then shrugged my shoulders, peering out at the still gaining ship.

The knight lightly elbowed my arm and chuckled, "It doesn't really surprise me that you didn't see it coming, those affected rarely do," he mused.

After a moment of silence, I reflected, "I think I might have noticed **something**, but with our task at hand..."

"You're too busy to even notice your own heartbeat, I know," the knight finished for me.

I nodded my head.

Loher suddenly and unexpectedly appeared at my side once again, holding another fresh mug of coffee, the smile was still shining upon her face.

"Thank you, Loher," I said with a slight song in my voice and smiled at her as I took the mug.

She continued to smile back, "Don't get used to this, McLaaud," she purred as she began to slowly walk away, glancing back at me once to see if I was still looking... I was.

The smaller ship was now almost at our side and only getting closer; I could easily see the orc pirates on board, growling, yelling and taunting with their fists pumping in the air, many wielding swords.

The Scorpion's Sergeant-At-Arms casually wafted about the ship, informing everyone to calmly get ready for the imminent clash with the enemy. "At de captain's signal, an' yoo'll **know** when ya sees it, we're all to turn an' attack de enemy, however ya sees dat'cha can... be ready!"

"I'm ready, are you?" Sir Quinn confidently asked.

"I am," I agreed and then slowly looked around the big ship to see who else would be ready.

Near the port-side bow, I located Balt and his Great Axe, near him to his left I saw Commander Vlad.

A whole line of elven archers began to spread out across the far side of the ship, while after a bit of a search, I located Loher way up top in the "Crow's Nest."

I have no idea how she got up there so quickly or how I didn't see her climb up the mast, but at least I knew that she was safe while being up there; quite deadly as well, as accurate as she is with her bow.

Meeka was standing at the starboard bow, chanting one of her ancient spells, but as hard as I looked, I could not find Brother Fost or Kuchoff anywh—

There was a tug on the leg of my pants.

I looked down to find the young Psionisist standing right behind me as we were positioned at the stern; he was staring up at me with that same goofy grin that I'm sure we have all, by now, grown to know and love.

The boy had saved all of our lives with his mysterious skill, countless times, and I was beginning to wonder just what kind of trickery he had in store for his newest set of 'subjects.'

"One can only wait and find out," I thought to myself.

I looked at the boy with a questioning gaze, "Have you seen Brother Fost?" I asked, nicely.

"Below deck," the child chimed and then began chanting one of his own ancient spells; I took a long pull from my now cold coffee and smiled.

As we waited for the captain's signal, I noticed that the orc pirates were preparing to attack us, and they were being quite obvious about it as well.

The sun was now high in the sky and the wind was very calm... almost too calm.

The two ships floated side-by-side and looked as if they were engaged in some sort of erotically seductive dance.

Several grappling hooks were rapidly tossed from the smaller of the two ships to the railing of ours; Captain Waxx then, finally gave the signal.

The orcs began to forcefully pull the two ships together as the other orc pirates attempted to cause mass confusion by yelling, screaming and banging on drums, gongs, and thin sheets of metal, creating an obnoxious cacophony.

Long wooden planks were then slid between the lashed together ships to create bridge-like walkways that connected the two.

———◆———

A dismal, gruesome conflict of metal-meets-flesh took place between the two ships, but we, the defenders, had the advantage of archers and wizards, something the orc raiders did not count on.

(We also outnumbered the orcs, four to one.)

Arrows, energy bolts and ice balls whizzed through the air overhead as they found their marks and targets with painful, if not deadly, accuracy.

It wasn't long until the sea surrounding the battleground turned red and was littered with the corpses of (mostly) orc raiders; shorter still when those corpses began to be consumed by all manner of ferocious sharks, making survival impossible if someone accidentally slipped and fell into the sea.

Each faction rushed in, to quickly board their enemy's ship as the onslaught continued.

I had made my way to the other ship, somehow unscathed, as Sir Quinn followed closely behind.

I turned to my left, just in time to see an arrow bury itself into the throat of an orc that was about to trounce me with his unarmed fists; I had to remind myself to thank Loher, once again, for saving my skin.

My attention was diverted away from the orcish pin cushion, by the familiar dwarven victory roar as Balt successfully vanquished yet another foe.

"How many is that for you now, Balt?" I asked above the noise of war, as I lopped off the head of an orc raider.

"Lost count after eight, meself. Wot's **yer** number?"

"That was my first," I called back. "Loher keeps pegging them off before I can even get close!"

"Love!" The dwarf wholeheartedly chortled and pounded his chest-plate with his free fist.

"**You've** noticed too?" I rhetorically asked and then looked to see if Loher was still there, watching my back.

She was no longer in the 'Crow's Nest' and I couldn't see if she was on deck, because The Scorpion's deck and rail rose high above that of the smaller ship.

The Scorpion looked huge compared to the subsequently tiny orc ship.

It occurred to me, as I studied the way the two ships were lashed together, that perhaps I should **cut** the ropes and free the mighty Scorpion.

"Balt! Sir Quinn!" I called, gaining their attention, "As soon as you can, get back to our ship!" I made sure they both saw me cut the first rope from one of the hooks.

The three of us safely made our way back aboard The Scorpion, just as another mixed volley of arrows, energy bolts and ice balls violated the smaller ship, claiming the lives of more of the dwindling orcish marauders.

As Balt and I started cutting more ropes, Sir Quinn and another Royal Soldier began pulling planks from between the two ships and stacking them aboard The Scorpion.

"They might come in useful," the knight said as they pulled the last plank.

There were only three ropes left to cut, when a chorus of terrified screams began to ring out from behind the enemy lines.

———◆———

The small orc ship violently slammed into the side of The Scorpion.

"What the—?" I wondered when I noticed that the sharks had suddenly vanished from sight, and I rapidly got this overwhelming feeling of dread.

The orc marauders stopped fighting and chiefly began to scramble onto the decks of The Scorpion, hacking away at the ropes that still bound the two ships together; the unmistakable look of fear was plainly written on their pig-like faces.

Members of both crews scattered and began to cower and hide, "What's happening?" I asked.

"Sea monster!" A sailor cowering behind a barrel whispered just loud enough for me to hear.

I quickly took a look around and noticed that the elven archers were taking full advantage of this lull to continue to peg off the orc raiders; they were completely unaware or unafraid of the apparent sea-dwelling horror lurking down below the waves.

The orc ship sharply bashed into the side of The Scorpion once again and then unexpectedly ...all was calm.

Several silent moments passed, everyone, including the archers stood still and looked frightened and/or confused.

"I got a **baaaad** feeling about this," I heard a voice say from behind me.

I thought to myself that I couldn't agree more.

After a while, one-by-one, the elven archers began to peg away at the orcs again, when unexpectedly, the water on the far side of the now drifting orc vessel violently exploded upward to reveal the surfacing image of what looked to be a giant humanoid hand made up of crystal clear, bluish-green seawater; time seemed to slow down enough for me to catch a quick glimpse of hundreds of fish swimming in the waters of the gigantic liquid hand.

"Ummm… Kuchoff?" I called out, "Are…**you** doing this?" I directed the question out into the air, not knowing where the young Psionisist was, hoping he had heard me.

"It's not me this time, McLaaud," his small, frightened voice answered from (again) directly behind me, as the aqueous hand curled up into an enormous dripping fist and plunged downward into the tiny orc ship.

(No one at this particular date in time was familiar with the term: 'When pigs fly,' but I'm quite sure that if the term **had** existed just then, people would be doing all of those things that they never thought they would ever have to do, because…)

Orcs were launched high up into the air from the sheer centrifugal force of the fist crushing the ship upon the surface of the water.

Sufficed to say, the orc ship was completely and utterly destroyed.

Huge chunks of splintered wood came crashing down upon The Scorpion, along with gallons upon gallons of seawater.

The aqueous hand rose up again, this time above The Scorpion.

It rose up higher and higher and then… it hovered for a moment.

Once again, time seemed to stand completely still for those of us that were bathed in the wavering shadow made by the monstrous hand-shaped menace.

❖

"Duratus Omnino!" I heard both Meeka from the bow and Kuchoff from the stern, conjure together as twin cones of a 'freeze' spell were cast up into the liquid hand shape above; the hand began to freeze, but would not stay solid.

"Salt water!" Brother Fost called out, now above decks, "It's made of salt water and won't freeze solid!"

The halfling priest sprinted from one wounded crewman to another, healing them as quickly as he could.

"Try to **boil** it!" I cried out.

Both wizards, still on opposite ends of the ship, changed their strategy as they called out, "Ignis!" at the same time.

Twin cones of a 'fire' spell were cast up into the hand shape above us and the hand began to boil and steam.

A cheer rose up from the decks of The Scorpion as the shape slowly drifted away in the breeze as clouds of vapor.

The cheer quickly became a horrified gasp as the steam began to take on its old shape of the seawater hand. (Sans fish.)

"Quickly, freeze the steam!" Sir Quinn excitedly suggested.

Meeka stopped casting her cone of flame and then called out the incantation for frost.

The 'freeze' spell shot up and engulfed the slowly forming steam-hand.

"Now what?" Kuchoff screamed in confusion.

"Someone else has to shatter the ice!" Meeka informed.

Loher and the rest of the archers launched off a well-aimed volley of arrows, but they were only bouncing off, "Cease fire!" Loher called, "Save your arrows."

"Oi!" Balt barked to gain Meeka's attention, "Aim it doon lower, Lass, so's I c'n get in a guid chop'r'two."

"What did he say?" Meeka asked above the noise of the spells.

"He said, 'aim it down lower so he can get in a good chop or two!'" Brother Fost translated.

Balt ran closer to the ship's railing as Meeka lowered her freezing cone and Kuchoff switched from fire to freeze; both wizards concentrated their freezing blasts at a lower level on the 'arm' of the creature that the dwarf could easily reach.

When Balt was finally satisfied that there was enough solid surface for him to chop, he let loose with a mighty swing and gracefully cleaved the frozen creature's arm in two, "**TIMBER!!**" Balt quipped as the semi- frozen beast's arm and hand toppled back into the water.

Another cheer rose from The Scorpion's deck.

"Quickly! Raise all of de sails, Mon!" Captain Waxx ordered, "Let's git outta dis area be'far de creature returns!"

The Scorpion jumped to life as if it had a life force of its own.

Kuchoff watched the main sail as it puffed with air from the light wind, "I have an idea!" He called out sharply, "Everyone, hang on!"

The young Psionisist quickly ran to the rear of the ship and as soon as all of the sails were down and puffed with wind, he drew in a great breath and called out the magical command: "Vento Flumine!"

A strong, continuous wind, quite like that of a tornado, was summoned and was suddenly crammed into the sails; The Scorpion almost literally **flew** across the water.

The boy was concentrating too much to give out a full smile, but we all could see one brightly shining from deep down within his doe-brown eyes.

Captain Waxx was the one who was **really** smiling, for two good reasons as well:

The first being, Kuchoff had saved The Scorpion from impending doom and the second reason being, the captain had never gone this fast with his ship before; he was pleasantly excited and having fun.

The young wizard's energy had been totally spent after just a few minutes, but the distance in which The Scorpion had traveled in such a short time was further than it would have gone in a day and a half at normal speed.

A thought had suddenly sparked within my mind that seemed worthy of entertaining, "The river we'll take to return to the harbor," I called out to anyone listening, "is it salt water or fresh water?"

"Fresh!" Brother Fost answered, "The river supplies most of the fish and useable water to—" The halfling stopped himself as he realized that he was about to give away the location of the hidden shire; I nodded my head at him to show that I understood.

"If that water creature attacks us again, I would like to make sure it does so in that river!" I announced.

"D'ye tink it will, Elf?" Balt queried.

"Indeed," I answered, "I'm sure you hurt it very badly, Balt, but I also believe that it is very much alive and very angry at us as well."

"How c'n ye be so sure I dinna kill ta beastie?" The dwarf asked, quite calmly, "Dinna ye see it drop doon like a stone?"

"I saw that," I admitted, "but I still think it was just too easy... Even for the mighty Balt Copperbottom!"

"T'was a bit too easy," Balt admitted with a chuckle and a half smile.

Almost as if on cue, the lookout in the 'Crow's Nest' shouted, "Ahoy! Sea monster astern, Captain!"

Meeka swiftly ran across the length of the ship loudly summoning, "Vento Flumine!" She aimed her full power into the sails.

Once again, the sails puffed out and almost ripped with the power as The Scorpion flew across the waves, outrunning the pursuing creature.

"Keep it going, Meeka!" I cried, "We're almost to the river!"

"A whole lot of good that river's gonna do us with both of our wizards out of energy and unable to cast the fire and frost spells." Sir Quinn grumbled.

"I'll see what I can do about healing them!" Brother Fost announced as he ran across the ship toward Kuchoff, who was just slowly rising to his feet, looking a bit stronger.

"Sir Quinn," I whispered into the knight's ear so no one else could hear, "we only need one wizard and Balt to kill this thing."

"Why did we need two before?" He asked, confused.

"They were trying to freeze salt water before. Salt water doesn't freeze well, so they had to turn it to steam first, before they could freeze it. The river is fresh water and doesn't need to be boiled, it will freeze on its own," I explained.

"Therefore, only one wizard, Kuchoff, is needed," Sir Quinn followed, "Balt can do the rest!"

"Exactly!" I agreed.

"Port!" The captain suddenly called out to the helmsman, "Hard ta port!"

The Scorpion started to turn left into the fresh water river, "Okay, Lady, dat be enough wind now!" The captain called out to Meeka, who in turn stopped her spell and The Scorpion began to slow.

Kuchoff, now wide-eyed and full of energy, stormed off to the back of the ship and began to chant one of the needed spells; Brother Fost went to go heal the wizard, Meeka.

A few moments later, and not a moment too soon, both wizards stood ready, willing and able, each chanting their own separate spell, determined to vanquish the beast of the sea.

"I thought we only needed one wizard for this?" Sir Quinn asked, whispering into my ear.

I shrugged my shoulders and smiled, "The more the merrier."

"Ahoy!" The lookout cried, "Sea monster astern again, Captain!"

We all looked directly behind us and not only saw the water-made hand of the creature, but exposed above the surface was the head, neck and chest to the belly of the ungodly beast.

The river was much too shallow to hide the humanoid water-man and we could plainly see all types of sea creatures within the giant frame; two recognizable parts of the water-man could be seen hovering within the massive form that were not fish or other aquatic creatures, they were the properly placed brain and beating heart.

For a moment we all stood staring, partially frozen in awe at the magnificent creature that we, unfortunately, had to destroy, before **it** could destroy **us**.

Commander Vlad called away our attention and spoke directly to the wizards, "I suggest that one of you freezes it while the other one blasts away at it with those energy bolts that you used against the dragon," he said, "**that** was impressive!"

"Perhaps they should aim for the heart and then the brain," I suggested and the two wizards agreed.

"We will be standing with arrows ready," Loher announced. "Archers, spread out at the back of the ship!"

She then gave me a look that suggested that I was included as well.

A moment later I noticed that even Brother Fost stood ready with his Blessed Crossbow, "Let's kick some liquid ass!" He said with a scowl.

The 'water-man,' now naval deep, gradually waded toward the slowly moving Scorpion.

"Steady..." the commander cautioned, "Wait for it to draw nearer..."

The creature moved closer, almost within range.

"Wait..." the commander began.

(The creature began to raise its massive fist...)

"...Aaaaannnd..." the commander continued.

(The fist rose higher...)

"...**NOW!**" The commander ordered as he brought his sword down, slicing thin air to show dramatic emphasis.

"Duratus Omnino!" Meeka summoned, the cone of ice launched up and violently slammed into the creature's chest, making it stagger back a few steps; the Water Elemental burbled out a gurgling shriek and began to clutch its rapidly freezing heart; as it did so, its hands and fingers began to freeze as well.

After a while, the commander moved closer to Meeka's side, "Move your cone to the creature's brain area, so the boy can get aim at its heart."

Meeka slowly moved her cone of ice across the creature's face to its brain, freezing everything in its path.

"Tela!" Kuchoff conjured, as a large energy bolt soared up with a loud droning hum and smashed into the freezing heart of the beast; a large chunk of the creature's chest popped off as smaller shards flew up and all around the impact zone.

The creature gradually slowed to a stop as Meeka's ice cone froze its face, head and brain; then, she ceased the spell.

"Tela! Tela! Tela!" The pair of wizards conjured together as ten separate, large energy bolts were launched, five at the frozen brain and five at the still slowly beating heart.

As the missiles impacted the frozen surface of the Water Elemental, the wizards both collapsed to the deck, exhausted.

Shards and chunks of ice, including the top of the creature's head, rained down upon The Scorpion and her crew, but the frozen monster still stood tall with its vitals now exposed.

"**Fire!**" Loher commanded, as a volley of arrows had been launched with stunning accuracy, both at the brain as well as the heart, but most of the arrows were harmlessly deflected.

"Use **flaming** arrows!" The commander cried out a suggestion.

"We'll need **fire** for that!" Brother Fost called out.

"Infiernus," Meeka weakly summoned just before she passed out for the final time.

The splintered debris of the orc's ship suddenly burst into flame on the deck by our feet.

"Thank – You – **Meeka!**" I sang out as we lit the tips of our arrows on the flames.

"Fire-at-will!" Loher offered as she let the first of many flaming arrows fly.

Before her arrow impacted, it was joined by several more, as a flaming volley found purchase in the heart and brain, melting the surrounding ice.

Amid the volley of flaming arrows, Brother Fost had taken special care and aimed with his Blessed Crossbow, squeezing the trigger...

...The bolt flew straight and true, finally nestling deep into the heart of the Water Elemental; the heart exploded!

(Exactly as if a blood-filled water balloon had been popped!)

Blood spurted out in raining gouts and began to pour down the frozen chest of the beast.

It flowed down in crimson rivulets that soon clouded up the river below, making it run a deep, dark red.

The creature's brain resembled a feathery porcupine, or perhaps a pin cushion.

"Is...is it...**dead?**" The halfling asked, opening his eyes.

"I believe it is." Commander Vlad laughed, mussing the priest's hair; and once again, a cheer erupted from The Scorpion's decks.

The sun had already begun to melt what was left of the ice statue and shortly, the head was completely gone.

The brain had fallen into the river with a large splash and we watched what seemed like a million fish quickly pick it apart and consume it before it ever had a chance to float downstream.

We had decided to drop anchor and rest there, so we could keep an eye on the place where most of the heart remained.

Not more than four hours of peace-filled rest later, the creature had completely melted away.

"We can go now," I announced, waking the dozing captain.

He looked at where the creature once stood, noticing it was gone, melted back into the sea, he agreed whole heartedly and the anchor was quickly raised.

Two hours and many, many songs later, we had moored up to the docks of North Port Royale.

Chapter Eleven

REVELATION

As soon as their feet made contact, Brother Fost and Balt dropped down to their knees and lovingly kissed the dry, solid ground, happy to be off that ship.

I had to admit, I too was glad to be on solid ground and out of the caves with the sun shining upon my face.

Captain Waxx and crew stayed aboard The Scorpion and bid us a fond farewell, until the next time we needed a ship.

We began to walk up the slowly inclining path that led to the gates of Salvus Hus.

We were tired, worn, battle fatigued, half-starved and by the looks we received as we walked through the gates, we must have looked worse than we felt.

"Unless the King himself stops you, speak to no one and go directly to your rooms," Sir Quinn announced as we passed by the guards and entered the castle, "We could all use some well-deserved sleep."

Twenty minutes later, I had my gear and boots stripped off and was just about to lie down on my bed when I heard a soft knock on my door.

Without even asking who was there, I opened the door to reveal the elven maiden, Loher, a weary smile upon her face.

"I gave my room to Kuchoff," she said. "I want to stay here, with you. Besides, I need some actual sleep; a reverie just won't do, as exhausted as I am. Like I told you once before," she gently pushed me to the side, entered my room and closed the door, "when I actually **do** sleep, I prefer **not** to do it alone."

I just stood there, silently trying to take in all of the information that was just fed to my weary mind, when she stripped off her own gear and washed up in the basin of water in the corner.

We both crawled into my bed and before I knew it, I found myself waking up after only a few hours of sleep; Loher was snuggled up to me, our legs and arms were entangled like snakes, and if I **had** wanted to move or get up without waking her, (which I didn't) it would have proved to be completely impossible.

I laid there, swimming around in my own thoughts, listening to her heartbeat and steady breathing.

Soon, I relaxed again and peacefully drifted off to sleep.

The next morning, I awoke to find Loher, fully dressed, beautiful, smiling, and standing beside my bed watching me.

I slowly opened my eyes and then she spoke, "I'm proud of you," she said as she swiftly leaned down and kissed my lips.

She smiled once again as she turned around and left the room.

"Get up!" I heard her call before the door could completely close.

I laid there for a few minutes longer, thinking about what might have been and then secretly thankful that I had not tried anything with her the night before.

I felt fortunate to have her as my friend and even more fortunate that, (for lack of a better term,) a love interest was slowly forming between us; I didn't want to mess that up or complicate it in any way, shape or form, her friendship was much too important to me to do that.

It didn't take me very long to get up, get dressed and get out the door.

***

As I walked down the empty marble hallway, looking for my companions, I suddenly realized that I was starving as the fragrance of cooking food invaded my senses and took over my free will.

I eagerly followed the scent of food to a large formal dining room that held a very large and long table made from a deep, rich, dark brown wood; the table seated at the very least, fifty people.

All of my companions were there, sat down and ready to enjoy a hearty meal.

"You're just in time," Meeka announced as I strolled into the room. "The food is just now being served, sit down," she said, as she patted the open seat between Loher and herself.

Ironically, that seat, I noticed only **after** I sat down, was directly across the table from none other than Sir Quinn, who cunningly shot me that infamous (secret) 'look'... 'Did you and Loher...??'

I gave him a smile, a raised eyebrow and a shake of my tilted head... 'I **could** have, but didn't.'

He wrinkled his brow and drew his cheeks up tight and quickly raised a single eyebrow... 'What stopped you?'

I yawned and tilted my head to my shoulder while closing my eyes... 'We were both too tired and fell asleep.'

The 'conversation' abruptly ended as the knight and I noticed Meeka and Loher staring at us curiously.

Sir Quinn quickly feigned a yawn, stretched and scratched his head in a feeble attempt to elude their suspicions.

I simply dug into the plate of food that was conveniently placed in front of me, "How was your night, Knight?" I asked between mouthfuls, trying not to smile.

"I slept like a log, how 'bout you?" He asked with a conniving grin.

I shot him the 'look'... 'Bastard!' "Like a log as well," I said, and then just for effect, I nodded my head a few times and then turned my attention to my breakfast.

I took pleasure in the knowledge that Sir Quinn was trying **very** hard not to break into a smile; he decided to half cover his face with his mug.

The rest of the meal went smoothly as the team idly conversed with each other, mainly about the past adventure.

I suddenly felt as if eyes were upon me, so I looked to my left to see if it had been Loher, but she and Meeka, who had moved across the table from the elven maiden, were engaged in a deep conversation about some sort of diet.

(Women...)

I continued to look around; Sir Quinn and Commander Vlad were throwing ideas around about a new industrialized form of farming...

(Hmmm...Mighty interesting....I don't think so!)

Brother Fost and Balt were, oddly enough, trying to figure out the differences between two cheeses.

My eyes finally settled upon the Psionisist, Kuchoff, who was eating a tomato, eyes wide and burning a hole into my very being.

He saw that I had finally noticed him, so he grabbed another tomato and slid down from his seat, took a big bite from his tomato as he scampered toward me.

"I guess it's almost time for me to go home," he said.

"I guess so," I said back, not knowing what else to say.

"I would really like to stick around and continue to help you and your team more, if I could," the boy offered.

"I'm not entirely sure what's going to happen, after we turn in the master map, the King may just send us **all** home," I told him.

He stood there, eyeing me curiously, nodding his head and then, as if an idea or an amusing thought had transpired, he smiled his toothy grin and quickly walked away, eating his tomato.

I watched him as he turned the corner and proceeded down a hallway, of which I had no idea where it led; I still sat there for a while, sipping on my coffee, drifting in and out of idle conversations, when finally, the King, joined by the Psionisist, appeared in the doorway that led to the throne room.

"Come," the King beckoned, "follow me, my friends."

We were all seated around the long table in the King's private chambers where the mission had originally begun.

This is the same place that Meeka and her pet white mouse had wowed and entertained us within a puff of pinkish smoke.

Seated around the table, headed by His Majesty, the King, Lagu Ofer'Eal was: To the King's right, Sir Seth Quinn, Brother Fost Atlberry, Meeka Ashpin and Balt Copperbottom.

To the King's left sat myself, (Thunor McLaaud,) next to me sat Loher D'Rolwynn, the young Psionisist Kuchoff Magnus and finally, the Royal Army's Commander Vlad Sleaner.

The remaining seats were occupied by a mixture of the three surviving Royal Soldiers, as well as the four surviving elven archers.

The master map, as well as a pile of the rough sketches, had been spread out across the table in front of the young King; we waited patiently while the King and his advisors studied the maps.

"Let me see if I understand this correctly," the young King began, "my Royal Army marched away from here, numbering fifty-six, correct?"

"That **is** correct, My Liege," Commander Vlad answered.

"Added to that, was what... sixty live lacerta?" The King asked.

"With all due respect, Your Highness," the commander responded, "it was only fifty-nine live lacerta."

The young King smiled at the bold correction, always pleased with accuracy, "Very well, Commander, fifty-nine live lacerta, making a total of," the young King paused to add up the total, "a convenient total of one hundred fifteen live soldiers, yes?"

"That is correct, my Liege."

The King rose to his feet and gazed around the table, taking a quick tally of us, "I see sixteen warm bodies gathered before me; are there any other survivors **not** present?" He regained his seat.

"Regretfully not, Your Highness," the commander replied.

The King scooped up a handful of the smaller maps and began shuffling through them, "Quite a lot of blood on these maps..." He got a thoughtful look in his eyes that rapidly turned to horror and then concern, "How many live, still, of the fifty-nine lacerta?"

"A total of eleven lacerta guard the dragon's treasure, your Highness," Sir Quinn announced and tapped his finger on a map showing Kusagi's grotto.

"I see..." the King murmured as he studied the blood soaked map. "The dragon, it is dead?"

"Yup!" Kuchoff happily announced with a proud giggle; Meeka moved to hush him.

The King raised a calm hand to stop her and smiled at the boy, half his own age.

After a moment's pause, the King simply uttered the word, "Treasure," and then lapsed back into thought, blindly eyeing each of us as his gaze circled the table and then returned to the maps.

A few more moments of pure silence passed until the King gained a glimmer in his eyes, "Am I to understand, my friends, that I now have a ship called The Scorpion under my command?" He asked excitedly.

This time, it was I that spoke, "That's not entirely accurate, my King," I began, "The Scorpion is commanded by Captain Mario Waxx, a pirate. Captain Waxx has agreed to **lend** us the use of his services... for payment, which has already been paid..., in full... indefinitely."

"Hmmm..." The King let his thoughtful voice trail off, once again, in deep thought.

His eyes darted from one map to another, to yet another, back and forth.

"Sooo... pray tell, what is the difference, Ranger?" The King asked without looking up from his maps.

I cleared my throat and began, "Captain Waxx is a pirate, you see, he will not obey anyone's orders, other than his own and I am sure he will outright **defy** any that may be directed at him; Captain Waxx **does**, however, respond very well to calm suggestions and bribes," I reported.

The King smiled at my words and slowly looked up from the maps, he let his eyes roam from one face to another, seeing us this time, until he had scanned each and every one of us, "Sixteen," he thought out loud, as he pushed his chair away and rose to his feet.

We all, out of respect, rose with him.

Without another word, the young King swiftly walked to the door, opened it and then, as an afterthought, turned around to face us once again, "If you so desire, you may go to the Royal Treasury and receive your payment. I will send word to your homes if and when your services are required once again, thank you." The King quickly turned on his heel and was joined by two guards and his advisors, as he exited the room, turned to the right and disappeared down the hall.

———◆———

"The apple never falls too far from the tree," the commander laughed and shook his head, as he strode to the door and disappeared to the left.

"What does **that** mean?" Kuchoff asked.

Sir Quinn put his hand on the Psionisist's shoulder and explained, "The **young** King is just like his father, the **old** King, before him."

"So we just... go home now?" The boy asked with a breaking voice.

"Well," Meeka chimed in, "we can't stay here."

"But, I have no home left to go to!" Kuchoff sniffled and suddenly began to cry.

Meeka quickly rushed to the boy's side and began to comfort him, "You can come home with me, back to Guadium," she soothed, "would you like that?"

The boy wiped his eyes with the back of his hand and nodded at the red haired magician.

"Then it is settled," she said, "my home is yours."

"Wot 'appened te yer 'ome, Laddy?" Balt asked.

"Destroyed," the Psionisist blinked and slid his small hand into Meeka's, "by hobgoblins a few days before the King's 'Call To Arms.' My mother was carried away by hobgoblins in the raid and my father was just killed in the cave by those damn olyame!" There was a waver in his voice.

Meeka held him close, "We will be family now," she soothed, "just you and me, okay?" She leaned down and gently kissed the top of the Psionisist's head; he began to smile.

By this time, the only people left in the room were us original six and Kuchoff.

"Oi!" Balt laughed, "Lucky seven!"

Meeka and I gave out a laugh.

"What are your plans now, Brother Fost?" Sir Quinn asked the priest.

The halfling sighed, "I will probably gather my effects from the room here I was occupying and return back to the Shire."

Balt unexpectedly broke into the conversation and made us all an offer that no one chose to refuse, "First place Meself is goin' be ta 'Broken Blade' fer a drink'r three an' yer all more'n welcome – nay – yer all **required** te join me," the dwarven fighter laughed. "Ye got's a hour te git yer sorry arses o'er t'ere!" With that, he swiftly stomped his way to the door, out and then to the left, soon followed by the priest and then the knight.

"Well," Meeka giggled, "I guess we'll meet you all at the 'Blade' in an hour."

"Where are we going until then?" Kuchoff asked as he gripped her hand a bit tighter.

"I, for one, would like to explore the rest of this castle, wouldn't you?" She asked, "It's not every day that you get free reign in a place such as this!"

"Yeah, let's go!" Kuchoff exclaimed; the new family walked through the door with big smiles and even bigger waves.

I turned to look at Loher as she just stood there smiling back at me, "What are **your** plans now that the mission is over?" I asked. Her only answer was a kiss.

Hand in hand, we walked through the door and followed our companions down the hall.

The hall stretched forward for approximately thirty-five normal walking strides and then turned to the left and went forward another four or five strides.

A vast chamber opened up before us, set in the same rich marble.

The large ornate door that led to the throne room was on our left, as the door that led out, to the courtyard was on our right.

As we exited the castle and entered the courtyard, the warm sun generously splashed upon our faces; I felt my knees weaken as my muscles melted in the warmth.

My blood ran warmer within my veins and the cold chill of fatigue slowly melted away as well.

The courtyard was vast and full of exuberant energy, as jesters, acrobats, clowns and mimes entertained the resident children of the lords, ladies and knights.

After taking a slow, roaming look around the grounds, I spied the young King himself, gazing down at the colorful show below his chamber windows.

A handful of knights, including Sir Quinn, were gathered near a tall, ancient oak tree, as Sir Quinn himself, told the other knights of our adventures passed, quite like an old codger; I **had** to laugh.

Sir Quinn saw Loher and I pass by, walking hand-in-hand, he gave me the 'look' once again, along with a brotherly smile and a wink; I rolled my eyes at him and then smiled and winked back.

It suddenly dawned on me, "I have to check on Stahvee," I told the elven maiden.

"Who?" She asked, as I swiftly but gently pulled her toward the stables.

As we entered, we had to pause at the door to let our eyes adjust to the darkness inside the stalls as opposed to the brightness of the sunshine outside.

As I took a few steps in, I mimicked a horse's nicker, which was instantly met with the familiar nicker, Stahvee's reply; Loher smiled with impressed appreciation.

Well!" Festus called out with a chuckle that slightly startled us, "Look who has returned!"

Loher composed herself and then grinned, "Hello, Festus," she said and then finally realized who Stahvee must be, "How's my Amarylis?"

Festus quickly looked us over and smiled at the sight of our joined hands, "Both of your horses are getting along very well," he said, "With each other, I might add." He swept his hand to a stall, "Quite the same as their owners, may I presume?" He smiled again.

As we looked into the indicated stall, we noticed that both of our horses, Stahvee, my black roan Stallion and Amarylis, Loher's appaloosa mare, were nuzzling each other. "I would almost call that 'love,'" Festus commented.

Loher looked directly and deeply into my eyes, smiled and simply whispered, "Perhaps it **is**."

I smiled back at her as I pulled out a few gold coins and handed them to the kind old man.

He thanked me, and then Loher and I took our leave of the stables.

Once outside, we drew Sir Quinn's attention away from the other knights, as I made an obvious motion toward the 'Broken Blade' and pantomimed a person taking a drink from a mug.

The good knight shot me the 'look'... 'I'll join you two in a moment.'

We turned and walked to the tavern in order to keep our appointment with Balt and the rest of our companions.

Once again, as we entered the tavern, much like we had to do at the stables, we paused for a moment to let our eyes adjust.

"I found the dwarf," Loher quietly announced, as she began to slowly lead me to our usual table in the far back left corner.

❖

The 'Broken Blade' was unusually busy for this particular time of the day.

Of the forty-three seats, only a dozen were empty, five of which were at the dwarf's table, the other seven were staggered about the room.

The fireplace was dark and cold, but fresh wood was set and waiting for night to arrive in just a few hours more.

The smell of cooked... fish, I think it may have been, was faint and growing ever lighter as the noon lunch hour also drifted further away, as the newer smells of pipe smoke and mead came in to replace it.

Groups of men and their mates were relaxing with drinks and various 'smokes,' with idle conversations dominating the quite pleasant atmosphere.

Sitting at another table in the far right corner, nearest the bar, I recognized two of the four elves as the 'lovers' from Dewarg's 'Ale House.'

The last non-human was an old elven male with long argent hair.

He sat alone in the darkened southwest corner, nursing a pint of fiery red... something I couldn't readily identify and enjoying an illustriously carved pipe.

Balt stood and smiled as we approached the waiting table, "Ye two lovebirds be ta first te arrive," he announced, grinning wildly as he stuck two fingers into the air and nodded at the advancing barmaid, "Ave yerselves a seat an' stay a spell, that is, if yer na in te much o' a hurry te git back te yer precious trees... are ye?"

I pulled out a chair and offered it to Loher, who smiled and graciously accepted, allowing me to push her in, closer to the table, "To tell you the truth, Balt," I said to the dwarven fighter as I took my own seat, "I'm not at all interested in getting back to my 'precious trees,' as you so finely stated, any time soon."

"Nor am I," Loher agreed.

The barmaid arrived with our drinks, "Ye might as well keep 'round here, Lass," Balt announced to detain her, "t'looks as if s'more o' me Mates'r 'bout te join us."

The barmaid glanced at the tavern's entrance, "Oh, you mean Seth?" She asked with a randy grin.

"Seth?" Loher and I whispered to each other in slight disbelief.

"Aye," Balt answered, ignoring our quip.

The barmaid began to walk back to the bar with a slight but noticeable new bounce in her step. "I **know** what **he** likes," she sang over her shoulder with a sly look in her eye.

"I bet you do," Loher giggled under her breath, as the knight strolled up to the table and took a seat.

"What's so funny?" He asked, as he noticed our feebly masked laughter, looking from face to face.

Balt smiled and shrugged his massive shoulders, as Loher and I tried to cover our own smiles with our drinks.

"The clouds are really beginning to roll in," Sir Quinn announced with genuine surprise in his voice, letting the previous question slither away into the darkness, unnoticed. "The wind has sure picked up as well!"

The barmaid returned to our table, Sir Quinn's drink in hand, that same, sly, almost wanton look continued to twinkle in her eye.

Sir Quinn shocked us all as he too gave the barmaid an amorous look, "Thanks, Billie."

Loher uncontrollably giggled into her drink again and quickly came up coughing; I'm not sure if she was faking the cough to cover up her second bout of laughter, but it was sure convincing to me if it **had** been fake, so to be on the safe side, I began to pat and rub her back.

"Are you okay?" Sir Quinn asked.

Loher closed her eyes and smiled under a fist that covered her mouth, as she coughed and nodded an affirmation to the knight.

Our halfling priest walked in, waving his hands around his head and face as if he was trying to shoo away some sort of flying pest. "I sort of ran into an old 'friend' of ours," Brother Fost announced, with an annoyed look upon his usually peaceful face.

As if on cue, Brendt, the sprite, hovered and then landed in the direct center of the table, "Ta-dah!" The sprite sang, splaying his arms wide open.

The barmaid, Billie, ambled back to our table to take the priest's order, either she didn't notice or didn't pay any attention to the sprite.

"I'll just have what he's having," Brother Fost said, as he aimlessly pointed at my mug; Billie nodded and walked away to get the order.

Brendt smiled, clapped his hands together once and magically, a small, sprite-sized cup made of amethyst appeared in his hand.

The sprite then reached over and dipped his cup into my drink, "Remember, half-Elf, you **owed** me," he winked, raised his full cup,

"Cheers!" He took a long pull, **"Ambrosia!"** The sprite exhaled in grandeur.

He dipped the amethyst cup again for a refill and then said, "This cup is made from what my ancestors called 'Amethystos,' which in our old language means: 'Not drunken.' My ancestors believed that the amethyst prevented intoxication."

He drained the cup and went back for thirds, "It's a good thing my cup is so small, huh?" He asked me with a wink, "Cheers!"

I leaned over to Loher and whispered, "What he said about amethyst just simply cannot be true."

"Why not?" She whispered back.

"That cup," I said, "is the same color as your eyes," I looked deeply into them, "They intoxicate me every time I look into them."

The elven maiden smiled, leaned closer and kissed me.

"Well, well, **well!**" The sprite exclaimed as he witnessed the kiss, "What do we have **here?**" Brendt stood smiling, wings fluttering excitedly and tapping his foot, his hands went to his hips.

"A budding flo'er," Balt mused, trying to smooth out his gruff voice.

"T'is a **wond'rous** thing!" Brendt laughed in approval, mocking the dwarf's rough accent.

"Get a **room!**" Meeka playfully hissed from the doorway as she guided Kuchoff in. "I hope we didn't miss much," she said, as she and the young Psionisist joined our table.

Sir Quinn stood up and offered the red haired magician his chair, the magic using duo sat down, and the valiant knight simply acquired a new chair from a different table.

Billie came back to our table once again to take yet another order, "Tis be ta total of us, Lass," Balt announced, "Let's make it a full eight drinkies."

Billie nodded and then raised a questioning eyebrow at the sprite.

Balt noticed the look and laughed, "Seven, ta wee sprite'll share off ta rest o' us."

Billie nodded once more and then quickly rushed back to the bar to fill the order.

I quickly took a look around the tavern and noticed that the four elves in the corner had gone, as well as a good number of the men.

Besides the eight members of our party, the old hoary elf in the dark corner and a small number of men and their women, that was all that remained.

Of the forty-three seats, now, twenty-nine were available.

"What was the weather like out there when you arrived, Meeka?" Sir Quinn asked in pure curiosity.

"That odd wind had finally died down, but it was almost as dark as night because of the cloud cover," she answered with a slight crease in her forehead and a crinkled up nose.

"It may help you to understand that there is only an hour of true daylight left in this day, if you don't mind an old elf cutting in," the elderly elf at the dark corner table added.

Then, with a seemingly simple wave of his hand, the once cold and dark fireplace sparked into bright and lively, roaring fire.

"Thanks, Avilyn!" The tavern's owner called from somewhere behind the bar.

"You're quite welcome, Lance!" The elderly elf (Avilyn?) called back.

"Avilyn?" I echoed his name in surprise as a question.

"That would be my name," he chuckled with a mysterious glint of some sort in his eyes.

"Named after the king of the dragons?" Sir Quinn breathed in awe.

The old elf suddenly burst forth with a whole hearted laugh that slightly shook the room and attracted everyone's attention, "No, my boy," he said, "that dragon was named…" He leaned forward and somehow looked us all right in the eyes, "…**BY** me."

"Huh??" Loher, Kuchoff and I gasped in an excited and yet unbelieving chorus.

The old elf pressed his right index finger to the side of his sharp, pointed nose, winked and slowly faded away into the shadows.

"That old codger sure is a gent to remember," Lance, the owner of the 'Broken Blade' laughed as he delivered our drinks, "he does that fire-lighting bit for me all the time."

"Who **is** he?" I asked my eyes still quite wide in amazement.

Lance only laughed again and shook his head, "Been coming in here as long as I've owned the place," he answered as he began to collect up all of the empty cups and mugs, "and longer still, as I can tell."

Lance glanced at the empty chair with a grin and shook his head as he walked back to the bar.

I found that I too, was staring at the dark corner in which the mysterious old elf had been sitting.

I wondered silently if he had either hidden in the shadows as Loher was so good at and so fond of doing, or if he had simply cast an 'invisibility' spell and was still there observing us, or if he had actually, magically gone away.

Loher drew my attention back to her as she gently placed her hand on my leg, under the table.

"…And **that's** why they call it a dimple!" Kuchoff said, completing the punch line to a joke I had unwittingly missed due to my being consumed within my own thoughts.

The rest of the team erupted into a hearty bout of jovial laughter; no one but Loher had noticed that I had not laughed, and I was thankful for that.

"Are you okay?" She asked in a whisper.

I smiled a genuine smile at her, "Yeah," I answered, "I was just lost in a thought about that old elf," I nodded at the dark corner.

The elven maiden smiled, and then we turned to face our friends.

"I would like to propose a toast!" I announced as I raised my cup, high above the table.

Brendt quickly filled his amethyst cup as well; the whole team joined in by raising their cups and mugs.

"To us and to the triumphant success of a mission completed and in good time!"

"Hear, hear!" They all replied in agreement.

"Cheers!" We all sang and took long pulls from our drinks... Together... As ONE.

EPILOGUE

T he celebration continued in the 'Broken Blade' as the unrelenting dark clouds rolled in, bringing an unnatural mist along with them.

The townsfolk of Salvus Hus quickly secured their homes for fear of a giant storm.

"Now I'd like te perpose a toast Meself," Balt announced as he climbed up to stand on the surface of the table, knocking empty cups and mugs, noisily to the floor; we all began laughing as the dwarf successfully accomplished this feat, "Te ta cap'n an' crew o' ta Scorpion! Wit'out them, we'd prolly **still** be walkin'!"

A cheer rose up from our table and we all started to applaud our fortunes, but as our applause died down, clapping from the tavern door continued...

My heart raced as I looked at the door, there, clapping, stood the vampire from the outskirts of Powell.

"I'm here to collect your debt, Ranger." The vampire growled in its in-human, wolf-like voice.

<The End>

If you enjoyed **Hollow** please post a review
and enjoy Thunor's continuing adventures in
Dark: Book Two of The Scorpion Chronicles.

www.ingramcontent.com/pod-product-compliance
Lightning Source LLC
Chambersburg PA
CBHW021154310726
48971CB00002B/631